THE TRAITOR

The Traitor

A Story of the Fall of the Invisible Empire

By

THOMAS DIXON, Jr.

Illustrated by

C. D. WILLIAMS

A FIREBIRD PRESS BOOK

Gretna 2001

Manufactured in the United States of America
Published by Pelican Publishing Company, Inc.
1000 Burmaster Street, Gretna, Louisiana 70053

DEDICATED TO
THE MEN OF THE SOUTH
WHO SUFFERED EXILE, IMPRISONMENT AND DEATH
FOR THE DARING SERVICE THEY RENDERED OUR COUNTRY
AS CITIZENS OF THE INVISIBLE EMPIRE

TO THE READER

This volume closes, as originally planned,
"THE TRILOGY OF RECONSTRUCTION"
"THE LEOPARD'S SPOTS"
"THE CLANSMAN"
"THE TRAITOR"

"The Clansman" ended with the political triumph of the Klu Klux Klan, or Invisible Empire. The story of "The Traitor" opens with the order of dissolution by General Forest and is set in the atmosphere of the fierce neighborhood feuds which marked the Klan's downfall in the Piedmont region of the South.

THOMAS DIXON, JR.

New York, 1907.

CONTENTS

BOOK I.

THE CRIME

THE TRAITOR

BOOK II.

A WOMAN'S REVENGE

CONTENTS

BOOK III.

PRISONER AND TRAITOR

LEADING CHARACTERS OF THE STORY

Scene: The Foothills of North Carolina.

Time: 1870 to 1872.

JOHN GRAHAM	Ex-chief of the Klan
MAJOR GRAHAM	His Father
BILLY	His Brother
ALFRED	The Family Butler
MRS. WILSON	Their Landlady
SUSIE	Her Daughter
DAN WILEY	A Mountaineer
STEVE HOYLE	Chief of the New Klan
JUDGE BUTLER	Of the U. S. Circuit Court
STELLA	His Daughter
AUNT JULIE ANN	His Cook
MAGGIE	Stella's Maid
SUGGS	A Detective
ACKERMAN	Of the U. S. Secret Service
ALEXANDER LARKIN	A Carpetbagger
ISAAC A. POSTLE	A Sanctified Man
THE ATTORNEY GENERAL	Of the United States
HON. REVERDY JOHNSON	Of Maryland
HON. HENRY STANBERY	Of Ohio
U. S. GRANT	The President

ILLUSTRATIONS

THE TRAITOR

Book I—The Crime

CHAPTER I

THE THREAT

W HAS the mather with the latch!"
John Graham stood in the soft Southern
moonlight fumbling over the gate of the old home-
stead from which the Civil War had driven his
family penniless.

"Used to be a latch anyhow, before his illus-
trious Dishonour, the Judge, and his African
Government, turned us out!" he continued to
mutter.

"Wonder if he's locked it? Didn't need bolts
for gates in our time—but he does—the old
Scalawag!"

Each word of the last sentence was slowly
hissed. Again he felt over the gate, tried both
sides without success, stepped back and surveyed
it critically.

"By Geeminy, the gate's grown up!—used to
be here—see the gravel walk on the other side."

He shook it gently.

"No mistake about it—grown solid to the fence. I'll have to climb over."

He touched the points of the sharp pickets, suddenly straightened himself with dignity and growled:

"I won't climb over my own fence, and I won't scratch under. I'll walk straight through."

A vicious lurch against the gate smashed the latch and he fell heavily inside.

He had scarcely touched the ground when a fair girl of eighteen, dressed in spotless white, reached the gate, running breathlessly, darted inside, seized his arm and helped him to his feet.

"Mr. John, you must come home with me," she said eagerly.

"Got to see old Butler, Miss Susie."

"You're in no condition to see Judge Butler." She spoke with tenderness and yet with authority.

"And why not?" he argued good-naturedly. "Ain't I dressed in my best bib and tucker?"

He brushed the dirt from his seedy frock coat and buttoned it carefully.

"You've been drinking," pleaded the girl.

"Yet I'm not drunk!" he declared triumphantly.

"Then you're giving a good imitation," she said with an audible smile.

"Miss Susie, I deny the allegation."

He bowed with impressive dignity.

Susie drew him firmly toward the street.

"You mustn't go in—I ran all the way to stop you in time—you'll quarrel with the Judge."

"That's what I came for."

"Well, you musn't do it. Mama says the Judge has the power to ruin you."

John's eyes shot a look of red hate toward the house and his strong jaws snapped.

"He has done it already, child!" he growled; paused, and changed his tone to a quizzical drawl. "The fact is, Miss Susie, I've merely imbibed a little eloquence on purpose to-night to tell this distinguished ornament of the United States Judiciary, without reservation and with due emphasis, just how many kinds of a scoundrel he really is."

"Don't do it."

"It's my patriotic duty."

"But you'll fight."

"Far from it, Miss Susie. I may thrash the Judge incidentally during our talk, but there will be no fight."

"Please don't go in, Mr. John!" she pleaded softly.

"I must, child," he answered, smilingly but firmly. "Old Butler to-day used his arbitrary

power to disbar me from the practice of law. If
that order stands, I'm a pauper. I already owe
your mother for two months' board."

"We don't want the money," eagerly broke
in the girl.

"Two months' board," he went on, ignoring
her interruption, "for my dear old crazy Dad,
helpless as a babe with his faithful servant Alfred
who must wait on him—two months' board for
my bouncing brother Billy, an eighteen-year-old
cub who never missed a meal—two months'
board for my war-tried appetite that was never
known to fail. No, Miss Susie, we can't im-
pose on the good nature of the widow Wilson
and her beautiful daughter who does the work
of a slave without wages and without a
murmur."

Susie's eyes suddenly fell.

"No, I've given Alfred orders to pack. We
must move to-morrow."

"You'll do nothing of the kind," cried the girl.
"You can pay us when you are able. Your
father saved us from want during the war. We owe
him a debt that can't be paid. He is no trouble,
and Alfred works the garden. Mother loves
Billy as if he were my brother. And we are
honoured in having you in our home."

The tender gray eyes were lowered again.

John looked at her curiously, bowed and kissed her hand.

"Thanks, Miss Susie! I appreciate, more than I can tell, your coming alone after me here to-night —a very rash and daring thing for a girl to do in these troublesome times. Such things make a fellow ashamed that he ever took a drink, make him feel that life is always worth the fight—and I'm going to make it to-night—and I'm going to win!"

"Then don't give old Butler the chance to ruin you," pleaded the gentle voice.

"I won't, my little girl, I won't—don't worry! I'll play my trump card—I've got it here."

He fumbled in his pocket and drew out a letter which he crushed nervously in his slender but powerful hand, drawing his tall figure suddenly erect.

The girl saw that her pleadings were in vain, and said helplessly:

"You won't come back with me?"

"No, Miss Susie, I've serious work just now with the present lord of this manor; my future hangs on the issue. I'll win—and I'll come home later in the evening without a scratch."

Again the slender white hand rested on his arm.

"Promise me to wait an hour until you are cooler and your head is clear before you see him —will you?"

"Maybe," he said evasively.

"If you do appreciate my coming," she urged, "at least show it by this; promise for my sake, won't you?"

He hesitated a moment and answered with courtesy:

"Yes, I promise for your sake, Susie, my little mascot and fellow conspirator of The Invisible Empire—good-bye!" He seized her hand, and held it a moment. "My! my! but you look one of us to-night, with that sylph figure robed in white standing there ghost-like in the moonlit shadows!"

"I wish I could share your dangers. I'd go on a raid with you if you'd let me," she cried eagerly.

"No doubt," he laughed.

"I'll sit up until you come," she whispered as she turned and left him.

John Graham leaned against the picket fence and watched intently the white figure until Susie Wilson disappeared. The talk with her had more than half sobered him.

"And now for business," he muttered, turning through the open gate toward the house. He stopped suddenly with amazement.

"Well, what the Devil! every window from cellar to attic ablaze with light. And the old scoundrel has always kept it dark as the grave."

He seated himself on a rustic bench in the shadows to await the lapse of the hour he had promised Susie, and pondered more carefully the plan of personal vengeance against Butler which was now rapidly shaping itself in his mind. That he had the power, as chief of the dreaded Ku Klux Klan, to execute it was not to be doubted. The Invisible Empire obeyed his word without a question.

Tender memories of his childhood began to flood his soul. Beneath these trees he had spent the happiest days of life—the charmed life of the old régime. He could see now the stately form of his mother moving among its boxwood walks directing the work of her slaves.

He had not been there before since the day her body was carried from the hall five years ago and laid to rest in the family vault in the far corner of the lawn. Ah, that awful day! Could he ever forget it? The day old Butler brought his deputy marshals and evicted his father and mother from the home they loved as life itself!

The Graham house had always been a show place in the town of Independence. Built in 1840, by John's grandfather, Robert Graham, the eccentric son of Colonel John Graham of Revolutionary fame, it was a curious mixture of Colonial and French architecture. The French touches were tributes to the Huguenot ancestry of his grandmother.

The building crowned the summit of a hill and was surrounded by twenty-five acres of trees of native growth beneath which wound labyrinths of walks hedged by boxwood. Its shape was a huge, red brick rectangle, three and a half stories in height, with mansard roof broken by quaint projecting French windows. On three sides porches had been added, their roof supported by small white Colonial columns. The front door, of pure Colonial pattern, opened directly into a great hall of baronial dimensions, at the back of which a circular stairway wound along the curved wall.

The attic story was lighted by the windows of an observatory. From the hall one could thus look up through the galleries of three floors and the slightest whisper from above was echoed with startling distinctness. The strange noises which the Negro servants had heard floating down from these upper spaces had been translated into ghost stories which had grown in volume and picturesque distinction with each succeeding generation. The house had always been "haunted."

The family vault in the remotest corner of the lawn was built of solid masonry sunk deep into the hillside. Its iron doors, which were never locked, opened through a mass of tangled ivy and honeysuckle climbing in all directions over the cedars and holly which completely hid its existence.

Popular tradition said that Robert Graham had loved his frail Huguenot bride with passionate idolatry, and anticipating her early death, had constructed this vault, a very unusual thing in this section of the South. It was whispered, too, that he had dug a secret passage-way from the house to this tomb, that he might spend his evenings near her body without the prying eyes of the world to watch his anguish. Whether this secret way was a myth or reality only the Grahams knew. Not one of the family had ever been known to speak of the rumour, either to affirm or deny it.

A year after his wife's death Robert Graham was found insane, wandering among the trees at the entrance of the vault. This branch of the family had always been noted for it's men of genius and it's touch of hereditary insanity.

On the day of his mother's burial John Graham had found his own father sitting in the door of this tomb hopelessly insane.

But he had not accepted the theory of hereditary insanity in the case of his father. The Major was a man of quiet courteous manners, deliberate in his habits, a trained soldier, a distinguished

veteran of the Mexican war, conciliatory in temper, and a diplomat by instinct. He had never
had a quarrel with a neighbour or a personal feud
in his life.

The longer John Graham brooded over this
tragedy to-night, the fiercer grew his hatred of
Butler. Something had happened in the hall the
day of his mother's death which had remained a
mystery. Aunt Julie Ann, who stayed with the
new master of the old house as his cook, had told
John that she had heard high words between
Butler and the Major, and when she was called,
found her mistress dead on the floor and his father
lying moaning beside her.

John had always held the theory that Butler
had used rough or insulting language to his mother;
his father had resented it, and the Judge, taking
advantage of his weakness from a long illness of
typhoid fever, had struck the Major a cowardly
blow. The shock had killed his mother, and
rendered his father insane. Experts had examined
the Major's head, however, and failed to discover
any pressure of the skull on the brain. Yet John
held this theory as firmly as if he had been present
and witnessed the tragedy.

He rose from his seat, walked to the front entrance of the house and looked at his watch by
the bright light which streamed through the

leaded glass beside the door. He had yet ten minutes.

He retraced in part his steps, followed the narrow path to the foot of the hill and entered the vault. Feeling his way along the sides to the arched niche in the rear, he pressed his shoulder heavily against the right side of the smooth stone wall forming the back of the niche, and felt it instantly give. The rush of damp air told him that the old underground way was open.

He smiled with satisfaction. He knew that this passage led through a blind wall in the basement of the house and up into the great hall by a panel in the oak wainscoting under the stairs.

"It's easy! My men could seize him without a struggle!" he said grimly, slowly allowing the door to settle back of its own weight into place again.

He stood for a moment in the darkness of the vault, clinched his fist at last and exclaimed:

"I'll do it!—but I prefer the front door. I'll try that first."

A few minutes later he had reached the house, knocked loudly and stood waiting an answer.

Aunt Julie Ann's black face smiled him a hearty welcome.

"Come right in, Marse John, honey, an' make yo' sef at home. I sho is glad ter see ye!"

John walked deliberately across the hall and sat

down on the old mahogany davenport under the
stairs behind which he knew the secret door opened.
He reached back carelessly, played with the spring
and felt it yield.

Aunt Julie Ann's huge form waddled after him.
"Fore I pass de time er day I mus' tell ye Marse
John, what de Jedge say. He give 'structions ter
all de folks dat ef any Graham put his foot ter dat
do' ter tell 'im he don't low you inside dis yard! I
tell ye, so's I kin tell him I tell ye—Cose, I can't
help it dat you brush right pass me an' come in,
can I, honey?"

"Of course not, Aunt Julie Ann."

Her big figure shook with suppressed laughter.
"De very idee er me keepin' Mammy's baby
outen dis house when I carry him across dis hall in
my arms de day he wuz born! An how's all de
folks, Marse John?"

"About as usual, thank you, Aunt Julie Ann.
How are you?"

"Poorly, thank God, poorly."

"Why, what's the matter?"

She glanced furtively up into the dim moonlit
gallery of the observatory and whispered:

"Dey wuz terrible times here las' night!"

"What happened?"

"Ghosts!"

"What, again?" John laughed.

"Nasah, dem wuz new ones! We got de lights all burnin' ter-night. De Jedge, he wuz scared outen ten years growth. He been in bed all day, des now git up ter supper. Wuz Marse William well las' night?"

"As well as usual, yes; Alfred put him to bed early."

"Well, sho's you born, his livin' ghost wuz here! He wuz clothed an' in his right min' too! I hear sumfin walkin' up in de attic 'bout leben erclock, an' I creep out in de hall an' look up, an' bress de Lawd, dar stood you Pa leanin' ober de railin' lookin' right at me! Well, sah, I wuz scared dat bad I couldn't holler. I look ergin an' dar stood yo Ma, my dead Missy, right side er him."

"Ah, Aunt Julie Ann, you were walking in your sleep."

"Nasah! I'se jist as waked as I is now. I try my bes' ergin ter holler, but I clean los' my breath and couldn't. So I crawl to the Jedge's room, an' tell him what I see. He wuz scared most ter death, but he follow me out in de hall an' look up. He seed 'em too an' drop down side er me er foamin' at de mouf. He's powerful scary any-how, de Jedge is—des like us niggers. I got him ter bed and poured er big drink er licker down 'im, an' when he come to, he make me promise nebber ter tell nobody, an' I promise. Cose, hit's des like I'se talkin' ter myself, honey, when I tell you."

"And this morning he gave orders to admit no one of the tribe of Graham inside the yard again?"

"Yassah!"

"Well, tell his Honour that I am here and wish to see him at once."

"Yassah, I spec he won't come down—but I tell 'im, sah."

She waddled up the stairs to the Judge's room. John heard the quarrel between them. Aunt Julie Ann's voice loud, shrill, defiant, insolent, above the Judge's. She served him for his money and her love for the old house, but secretly she despised him as she did all poor white trash and in such moments made no effort to hide her feelings.

"Bully for Aunt Julie Ann!" John chuckled.

When she returned, he slipped the last piece of money he possessed into her hand and smiled.

"Keep it for good luck," he said.

"Yassah! De Jedge say he be down as soon as he dresses—he all dress now but he des want ter keep you waitin'."

"I understand," said John with a laugh. "Are you sure, Aunt Julie Ann, that the ghost of the

Major you saw last night wasn't the real man himself?"

"Cose I'se sho'. Hit wuz his speret!"

"Alfred says he's walking in his sleep of late; at least he found mud on his shoes the other morning when he got up."

"De Lawd, Marse John, hit wuz his speret, des lak I tell ye. He didn't look crazy no mo'n you is. He look des lak he look in de ole days when we wuz all rich 'an' proud and happy. He wuz laughin' an' talkin' low like to my Missy an' she wuz laughin' an talkin' back at 'im. I seed 'em bof wid my own eyes des ez plain ez I see you now, chile."

"You thought you did, anyway."

"Cose I did, honey. De doors is all locked an' bolted wid new iron bolts—nuttin but sperets kin get in dis house atter dark—de Jedge he sees 'em too—des ez plain ez I did."

"And this coward is set to rule a downtrodden people," John muttered fiercely under his breath. "Yes it's easy, he'll do what I tell him to-night, or —I'll—use—the—power I wield—to—execute— the—judgment—of—a—just—God."

"What you say, honey?" Aunt Julie Ann asked.

"Nothing."

"Dar's de Jedge commin' now," she whispered, hastily leaving.

John kept his seat in sullen silence until the shuffling footsteps of his enemy had descended the stairs and crossed half the space of the hall.

The younger man rose and gazed at him a moment, his eyes flashing with hatred he could no longer mask.

The Judge halted, moved his feet nervously and fumbled at the big gold watch-chain he wore across his ponderous waist. His shifting bead eyes sought the floor, and then he suddenly lifted his drooping head like a turtle, approached John, in a fawning, creeping, half-walk, half-shuffle, and extended his hand.

"I bid you welcome, young man, to the old home of your ancestors. In fact, I'm delighted to see you. I heard to-day that you would probably call this evening, and had the servants illuminate every room in your honour."

"Indeed!" John sneered.

"Yes, I've wished for some time that I might have such an opportunity to talk things over with you."

John had turned from the proffered hand and seated himself with deliberate insolence.

"Thanks for the illuminations in honour of my family!"

The sneer with which he spoke was not lost on the Judge. His patronising judicial air, so newly acquired, wavered before the cold threat of the younger man's manner. Yet he recovered himself sufficiently to say:

"My boy, I like your high spirit, but I *must* give you a little fatherly advice."

"Seeing that my own father at present cannot do so."

The Judge ignored the interruption and seated himself with an attempt at dignity.

"Mr. Graham, you must recognise the authority of the United States Government."

"Which means you?"

"I was compelled to make an example of disloyalty."

"You disbarred me from personal malice."

"For your treasonable utterances."

"I have the right to criticise your degradation of the judiciary in using it to further your political ambitions."

"I disbarred you for treason and contempt of court."

John rose and stood glaring at the judge whose shifting eyes avoided him.

"Well, you're on solid ground there, your Honour! Were I the master of every language of earth, past master of all the dead tongues of the ages, a genius in the use of every epithet the rage of man ever spoke, still words would have no power to express my contempt for you!"

The Judge shuffled his big feet as if to rise.

"Sit still!" John growled. "I've come here to-night to demand of you two things."

"You're in no position to demand anything of me!" spluttered Butler, running his hand nervously through his heavy black hair.

"Two things," John went on evenly: "First revoke your order and restore me to my law practice to-morrow morning."

"Not until you apologise for your criticism."

"That's what I'm doing now. I profoundly regret the incident. I should have kicked you across the street—criticism was an error of judgment."

Butler shambled to his feet, trembling with rage, pulled nervously at his beard again and gasped:

"How dare you insult me in my house!"

"It's my house!" flashed the angry answer.

"Your house?" the Judge stammered, again tugging at his beard.

"Yes, sit down."

The astonished jurist dropped into his chair, his shifting basilisk eyes dancing with a new excitement.

"Your house, your house—why, what—what!"

"Yes and you're going to vacate it within two weeks."

"What do you mean, sir?" demanded the Judge, plucking up his courage for a moment.

"I mean that the distinguished jurist, Hugh Butler, who had the honour of presiding over the trial of Jefferson Davis, and now aspires to the leadership of his party in the South, was living in a stolen house when he delivered his famous charge concerning traitors to the grand jury, that morning in Richmond. It is with peculiar personal pleasure that I now brand you to your face —coward, liar, perjurer, thief!"

John paused a moment to watch the effects of his words on his enemy. The cold sweat began to appear in the bald spot above the Judge's forehead, and his answer came with gasping feeble emphasis:

"I bought this house and paid for it!"

"Exactly!" sneered the younger man. "But I never knew until I got this letter"—he drew the letter from his pocket—"just how you came to buy a house which cost $50,000 for so trifling a sum of money."

"Who wrote that letter?" interrupted the Judge eagerly.

"Evidently a friend of yours, once high in your councils, who has grown of late to love you as passionately as I do. And I think he could put a knife into your ribs with as much pleasure."

The Judge winced and glanced nervously into the galleries.

"Don't worry, your Honour. If you take the medicine I prescribe, amputation will not be necessary. Let me read the letter. It's brief but to the point:

To JOHN GRAHAM, ESQ.

Dear Sir: The secret of Butler's possession of your estate is simple. Under his authority as United States Judge, he ordered its confiscation, forced his wife to buy it for $2,800, at a fake sale, which had not been advertised, and later had it reconveyed to him. His wife refused to live in the house, sent her daughter to school in Washington, and died two years later from the conscious dishonour she had been obliged at least in secret to share. A suit brought before the United States Supreme Court will restore your property, hurl a scoundrel from the bench, and cover him with everlasting infamy.

A FORMER PAL OF HIS HONOUR.

"An anonymous slanderer!" snorted the Judge.

"Yet he expresses himself with vigour and accuracy, and his words are backed by circumstantial evidence."

Butler sprang to his feet livid with rage crying: "John Graham, you're drunk!"

"Just drunk enough to talk entertainingly to you, Judge."

"Will you leave my house? or must I call an officer to eject you, sir?" he thundered.

"A process of law is slow and expensive, Judge," said John with a drawl. "I haven't the money at present to waste on a suit. May I ask when you will vacate this estate?"

"When ordered to do so by the last court of appeal, sir!"

John looked the Judge squarely in the eye and slowly said:

"You are before the last court of appeal now, and it's judgment day."

"I understand your threat, sir, but I want to tell you that your Ku Klux Klan has had its day. The President is aroused—Congress has acted. I'll order a regiment of troops to this town to-morrow! Dare to lift the weight of your little finger against my authority and I'll send your crazy old father to the county poorhouse and you to the gallows—to the gallows! I warn you!"

John took a step closer to his enemy, towering over his slouchy figure menacingly, and said·

"When will you vacate this house?"

Butler grasped the back of his chair, trembling with fury.

"The possession of this estate is the fulfillment of one of the proudest ambitions of my life."

"When will you get out?"

"And my daughter has just returned to-day from Washington, a beautiful accomplished woman, to preside over it."

"When—will—you—get—out?"

"When ordered by the Supreme Court of the United States—or when I'm carried out—feet—foremost—through—that—door!"

The Judge choked with anger.

"Then, until we meet again!"

John bowed with mock courtesy, walked across the hall to the alcove and took his hat from the rack where Aunt Julie Ann had hung it, just as Stella Butler sprang through the rear entrance with a joyous shout, reached at a bound the Judge's side and threw her arms around his neck.

"Oh! Papa, what a glorious night! Steve and I had such a ride!" The Judge placed his hand on her lips and whispered:

"My dear, there's someone here."

Stella glanced over her shoulder and saw John fumbling his hat in embarrassment.

"Why it's the famous Mr. John Graham—introduce me, quick!"

"Not to-night, dear; I do not wish you to know him."

Stella released herself and, with a ripple of girlish laughter, walked boldly over to John, her face wreathed in friendly smiles.

"Mr. Graham, permit me to introduce myself, Stella Butler. My father has just forbidden it. I care nothing for your old politics—shall we not be friends?"

She extended a dainty little hand and John took it stammering incoherently. Never had he touched a hand so warm and tender and so full of vital magnetism. It thrilled him with strange confusion.

Never had he seen a vision of such bewildering loveliness. An exquisite oval face with lines like a delicate cameo, cheeks of ripe-peach red, a crown of unruly raven-black hair, and big brown eyes shaded by heavy lashes. Her dress showed the perfection of good taste and careful study—a yellow satin, trimmed in old lace that fitted her rounded little figure without a wrinkle, dainty feet in snow-white stockings and bow-tipped slippers that peeped in and out mischievously as she walked, and with it all a magnetic personality which riveted and held the attention.

He stared at her a moment dumb with wonder. Could it be possible that a girl of such extraordinary beauty, of such remarkable character, of such appealing manners could have been born of such a father!

"As the new mistress of your old home let me bid you a hearty welcome, Mr. Graham," she said softly. "You must come often and tell me all its legends and ghost stories?"

The Judge shuffled uneasily and cleared his throat with nervous anger.

"Now keep still, Papa! I'm going to make this old house ring with joy and laughter. I won't have any of your political quarrels. I'm going to be friends with everybody, as my mother was—they say she was a famous belle in her day, Mr. Graham?"

"So I have often heard," John answered with increasing confusion, as he retreated toward the door.

"You will come again?"

"I hope to soon," he gravely answered as he bowed himself out the door.

CHAPTER II

STEVE HOYLE had called early at the Judge's to see Stella the morning after John's encounter in the hall. As he paced restlessly back and forth waiting the return of Stella's maid, he was evidently in an ugly humour.

When he heard the story at the hotel late the night before, that his hated rival in politics and society had dared to venture into Judge Butler's home, he could not believe it. And the idea that Stella should receive him had cut his vanity to the quick.

The richest young man in the county, he aspired to be the most popular, and he had long enjoyed the distinction in the estimation of his friends of being the handsomest man in his section of the state. In his own estimation there had never been any question about this. And beyond a doubt he was a magnificent animal. Six feet tall, a superb figure, somewhat coarse and heavy in the neck, with smooth, regular features. He was slightly given to fat, but his complexion was red and clean as a boy's, and he might well be pardoned his vanity when one remembered his money.

His father, the elder Hoyle, who had avoided service in the war by hiring a substitute, had emerged from the tragedy far wealthier than when he entered it. Some people hinted that if the Treasury Agents, who had stolen the cotton of the country under the absurd and infamous Confiscation Act of Congress, would speak, they might explain this fortune. They had never spoken. The old fox had been too clever and his tracks were all covered.

Steve had recently met Stella at one of her school receptions in Washington while on business for his father, yielded instantly to her spell, and they were engaged. He felt that he had condescended to honour the Judge by marrying into his family.

Butler never had been a slave owner, and in spite of his fawning ambitions as a turncoat politician and social aspirant, he was still poor— so poor in fact that he could scarcely keep up appearances in the Graham mansion. Steve planned to live there after his marriage in a style befitting his wealth and social position. He noted the faded covering on the old mahogany furniture and determined to make it shine with new plush on his advent as master.

He walked over to the hall mirror and adjusted his tie. He was getting nervous. Stella was keeping him waiting longer than usual. She was doing this to tease him, but he would have his revenge when they were married.

Steve had quickly come to a perfect understanding with the Judge. The Piedmont Congressional District, which included several mountain counties, was overwhelmingly Democratic. The Judge, as the Republican leader, had promised Steve to put up no candidate, but to support him as an independent if the approaching Democratic Convention nominated John Graham for Congress.

Steve as a man of capital proclaimed that the money interests of the North should be cultivated and that a deal with the enemy was always better than a fight.

Sure of his success, he had already promised Stella with boastful certainty a brilliant social season in Washington as his wife. In spite of his immense vanity, he knew that this promise had gone far to win her favour. She too was vain of her beauty, and her social ambitions were boundless. He had received her mild professions of love with a grain of salt. She was yet too young and beautiful to take life seriously. His fortune and his good looks had been the magnets that drew her. But he was content. He would make

her love him in due time. He was sure of it.
Yet on two occasions he had observed that she had
shown a disposition to flirt skilfully and daringly
with every handsome fellow who came her way—
and it had distressed him not a little.

He was angry and uneasy this morning, and
made up his mind to assert his rights with dignity
—and yet with a firmness that would leave no
question as to who was going to be master in his
house. He decided to nip Stella's acquaintance
with John Graham in the bud on the spot. That
he had called for any other reason than to see her,
never occurred to him.

When Maggie, Stella's little coal black maid, at
length reappeared, she was grinning with more
than usual cunning.

"Miss Stella say she be down in a minute,"
she said with a giggle.

"You've been gone a half hour," Steve answered
frowning.

"I spec I is," observed Maggie, continuing to
giggle and glance furtively at Steve.

"What's the matter with you?" he asked
suspiciously.

"Nuttin."

He held up a quarter and beckoned. She
hastened to his side.

"I want us to be good friends."

She took the money, grinned again and said:
"Yassah!"

"Now, what have you been giggling about?"

"Mr. John Graham wuz here last night!"

"So I hear. Did he see Miss Stella?"

"Deed he did! Dat's what dey all come fur.
She so purty dey can't hep it."

"How long did he stay?"

"Till atter midnight!"

"Indeed!"

"Yassah!" Maggie went on, walling her eyes
with tragic earnestness. "She play de pianer
fur 'im long time in de parlour, an' he sing fur
her an' den she sing fur him."

Steve cleared his throat angrily.

"Yassah! an' atter dey git froo singin' she take
him out fur er stroll on de lawn an' dey go way
down in de fur corner an' set in one er dem rustics
fur 'bout er hour. Den dey come in an' bof un
'em set in de moonlight in de hammock right close
side an' side, and he talk low an' sof, an' she laugh,
an' laugh, an' hit 'im wid er fan—jesso! Yassah.
Sh! She comin' now!"

The girl darted out of sight as Stella's dress
rustled in the hall above.

Steve pulled himself together with an effort, and
met her at the foot of the stairs.

She made an entrancing picture as she slowly

descended the steps, serenely conscious of her beauty and its power over the man below whose eyes were now devouring her. The flowing train of her cream-coloured morning gown made her look a half foot taller than she was. She had always fretted at her diminutive stature, and wore her dresses the extreme length to give her added height.

With a gracious smile she welcomed Steve and he attempted to kiss her. She repulsed him firmly and allowed him to kiss her hand.

"Stella dear," he began petulantly, with an accent of offended dignity, "you must quit this foolishness! We have been engaged three weeks and I've never touched your lips."

She laughed and tossed her pretty head.

"And we're engaged!"

"Not yet married," she observed, lifting her arched brows.

"I have honoured you with my fortune and my life."

"Thanks," she interrupted smiling.

Steve flushed and went on rapidly.

"Really, Stella, the time has come for a serious talk between us."

She seated herself at the piano and ran her fingers lightly over the keys. Steve followed, a frown clouding his smooth handsome forehead.

"Will you hear me?" he asked.

"Certainly!" she answered, turning on him her big brown eyes. In their depths he might have seen a sudden dangerous light, had he been less absorbed in himself. As it was he only saw a smile lurking about the corners of her lips which irritated him the more.

"I understand that John Graham called on you last night?"

"Indeed, I hadn't heard it," she answered lightly.

"And stayed until after midnight."

Stella sprang to her feet, looked steadily at Steve, frowned, walked to the door and called:

"Maggie!"

The black face appeared instantly.

"Yassum!" she answered, with eager innocence.

"Have you said anything about Mr. Graham's visit last night?"

Maggie walled her eyes in amazement at such an outrageous suspicion.

"No, M'am! I aint open my mouf—has I Mister Steve?"

"Certainly not," Steve answered curtly.

"I thought I heard your voice in the hall," Stella continued, looking sternly at Maggie.

"Nobum! Twan't me. I nebber stop er second.

I pass right straight on froo de hall—nebber even look t'ward Mr. Steve."

"You can go," was the stern command.

"Yassum!" Maggie half whispered, backing out the door, her eyes travelling quickly from Steve to her mistress.

"As my affianced bride," he went on firmly, "I cannot afford to have you receive the man who is my bitterest enemy." ·

With a smile, Stella quickly but quietly removed the ring from her hand and gave it to Steve, who stood for a moment paralysed with astonishment.

"Stella!" he gasped.

"The burden of your affianced bride is too heavy for my young shoulders."

"Forgive me dear!" he pleaded.

"I prefer to receive whom I please, when and where I please, without consulting you. When I need a master to order my daily conduct, I'll let you know.

"But, Stella, dear!"

"Miss Butler—if you please!"

"I—I only meant to tell you that I love you desperately, that I'm jealous and ask you not to torture me—you cannot mean this, dear?"

"How dare you address me in that manner again!" she cried, flaming with anger, the tense little figure drawn to its full height.

Steve attempted to take her hand, but the fierce light in her eyes stopped him without a word.

"Leave this house instantly!" she said, with quiet emphasis.

With deep muttered curses in his soul against John Graham, Steve turned and left.

As he passed through the doorway, a black face peeped from the alcove and giggled.

CHAPTER III

A BLOW IS STRUCK

TRUE to his word Butler called for a regiment of United States troops.

On the second day after his interview with the Judge, John Graham watched from his office window the blue coats march through the streets of Independence to their camp.

He turned to his chair beside a quaint old mahogany desk and wrote an official order to each of the eight district chiefs of the Invisible Empire who were under his command in the state.

When he had finished his task he sat for an hour in silence staring out of his window and seeing nothing save the big brown eyes of a beautiful girl—eyes of extraordinary size and brilliance that seemed to be searching the depths of his soul. It was a new and startling experience in his life. He had made love harmlessly after the gallant fashion of his race to many girls; yet none of them had found the man within.

He was angry with himself now for his inability to shake off the impression Stella Butler had made. He hated her very name. The idea of his ever seeking the hand of a Butler in marriage made him shiver. To even meet her socially with such a father was unthinkable. And yet he kept thinking.

Two things especially about her haunted him with persistence and had thrown a spell over his imagination—the strange appealing tenderness of her eyes and the marvellous low notes of her voice, a voice at once musical, and warm with slumbering passion. Her voice seemed the echo of ravishing music he had heard somewhere, or dreamed or caught in another world he fancied sometimes his soul had inhabited before reaching this. Never had he heard a voice so full of feeling, so soft, so seductive, so full of tender appeal. Its every accent seemed to caress.

He cursed himself for brooding over her and then came back to his brooding with the certainty of fate. Yet it should make no difference in his fight with old Butler. He would kick that fawning, creeping scoundrel out of his house if it was the last and only thing he ever accomplished on earth. The only question he still debated was the time and method of the execution of his plan.

One thing became more and more clear—he was going to need the full use of every faculty with which God had endowed him and he must set his house in order.

He opened the door of the little cupboard above his desk and took from it a decanter of moonshine whiskey Dan Wiley, one of his mountain men, had always kept filled for him. From the drawer he took two packs of cards and a case of poker chips. The cards and chips he rolled in a newspaper, placed in his stove and set them on fire. He smiled as he stood and listened to the roar of the sudden blaze. He raised his window and hurled the red-eyed decanter across the vacant lot in the rear of his office and saw it break into a hundred fragments on a pile of stones.

"Wonder what Dan will say to that when he comes this morning?" he exclaimed, looking at his watch and resuming his seat.

He heard a stealthy footfall at the door, turned and saw the tall lanky form of the mountaineer smiling at him.

"Well, Chief, you sent for me?"

"Yes, come in Dan!"

Dan Wiley tipped in and stood pulling his long moustache thoughtfully, before taking a chair.

"What's on your mind?" asked John.

"I heered somethin'."

"About me?"

"Yes, and it pestered me."

"Well?"

"They say you got drunk night 'fore last."

"And you're going to preach me a sermon on temperance, you confounded old moonshining distilling sinner!"

"Ye mustn't git drunk," observed Dan seriously.

"But, didn't you bring me the whiskey?"

"Not to git drunk on. I brought it as a compliment. My whiskey's pure mountain dew, life restorer—it's medicine."

"It's good whiskey, I'll say that," said John. "Even if you don't pay taxes on it. You brought the men?"

"Yes, but Chief, I'm oneasy."

"What about?"

"Don't like the looks er them dam Yankees. I'm a member er the church an' a law abidin' citizen."

"Yet I hear that a revenue officer passed away in your township last fall."

"Rattlesnakes and Revenue officers don't count —they ain't human."

"I see!" laughed John.

"Say," Dan whispered, "you ain't calculatin' ter make a raid ter-night with them thousand bluecoats paradin' round this town, are ye?"

"That's my business, Dan," was John's smiling answer. "It's your business as a faithful nighthawk of the Empire to obey orders. Are you ready?"

"Well, Chief, I followed you four years in the war, an' I've never showed the white feather yet, but these is ticklish times. There's a powerful lot er damfools gettin' ermongst us, an' I want ter ax ye one question?"

"What?"

"Are ye goin' ter git drunk ter-night?"

John walked to Dan's side and placed his hand on his shoulder, and said slowly:

"I'll never touch another drop of liquor as long as I live. Does that satisfy you?"

"I never knowd a Graham ter break his word."

John pressed the mountaineer's hand.

"Thanks Dan."

"I'm with you—and I'll charge the mouth of the pit with my bare hands if you give the order."

"Good. Meet me at the spring in the woods behind the old cemetery at eleven o'clock to-night with forty picked men."

"Forty!—better make it an even thousand, man for man with the Yanks."

"Just forty men, mark you—picked men, not a boy or a fool among them."

"I understand," said Dan, turning on his heel toward the door.

"And see to it"—called John—"I want them mounted on the best horses in the county and every man armed to the teeth."

Dan nodded and disappeared.

By eight o'clock the town was in a ferment of excitement and the streets were crowded with feverish groups discussing a rumour which late in the afternoon had spread like wild-fire. From some mysterious source had come the announcement that a great Ku Klux parade was to take place in Independence at midnight for the purpose of overawing if not attacking the regiment of soldiers, which had just been quartered in the town.

By eleven o'clock the entire white population, men, women and children, were crowding the sidewalks of the main street.

Billy Graham passed John's office with Susie Wilson leaning on his arm. Billy was in high feather and Susie silent and depressed.

"Great Scott, Miss Susie, what's the matter? This isn't a funeral. It's a triumphant demonstration of power to our oppressors."

"I wish they wouldn't do it with all these troops in town," answered the girl, anxiously glancing at the dark window of John's office.

"Bah! The Ku Klux have been getting pusillanimous of late—haven't been on a raid in six months. They need a leader. Give me a hundred of those white mounted men and I'd be the master of this county in ten days!"

"It's a dangerous job, Billy."

"That's the only kind of a job that interests me. A dozen wholesome raids would put these scalawags and carpetbaggers out of business. There ought to be five thousand men in line to-night. I'll bet they don't muster a thousand. It wouldn't surprise me if they backed out altogether."

"I wish they would," sighed Susie.

"Of course you do, little girl," said Billy with sudden patronising tenderness. "I know what you need."

Susie smiled and asked demurely:

"What?"

Billy seized both her hands and drew her under the shadow of a tree.

"A strong manly breast on which to lean—Susie, my Darling, I love you! Will you be my wife?"

Susie burst into a fit of laughter and Billy dropped her hands in rage.

"You treat the offer of my heart as a senseless joke, young woman?"

"No, Billy dear, I don't. I appreciate it more than words can express. You have paid me the highest tribute a girl can receive, but the idea of marrying a boy of your age is ridiculous!"

"Ridiculous! Ridiculous! How dare you

insult me? I'm as old as you are!" thundered
Billy.

"Yes, we are each eighteen."

"And your mother married at sixteen."

"And she's still only sixteen," said the girl
with a sigh.

"Wait a few days and I'll show you whether
I'm a man or not," said Billy, with insulted dignity. "Come, your mother is waiting for us at
the corner."

Mrs. Wilson stood among a group of boys
chatting and joking. She belonged to the type
of widows, fair, fat and frivolous. Time had
dealt gently with her. She was still handsome
in spite of her weight, and intensely jealous lest
her serious daughter supplant her in the affections
of the youth of Independence.

She greeted Billy with just the words to heal his
wounded vanity.

"My! Billy, but you look serious and manly!
I'd kiss you if the other boys were not here. You
ought to be at the head of that line of white raiders
to-night"—she dropped her voice to a whisper—
"I'll be making your disguise before long."

Billy turned from Susie and devoted himself
with dignity to her mother.

The widow lifted her hand in sudden warning.

"Sh! Billy, the enemy! There goes Stella Butler

with that fat little detective whom the Judge has imported with the troops."

"Captain" Suggs of the Secret Service was more than duly impressed with his importance as he forced his pudgy figure through the throng on the sidewalk, ostentatiously protecting Stella from the touch of the crowd.

"It's arrant nonsense, Miss Stella," he was saying, as they passed. "These Southern people are savages, I know——"

"Why, Captain, I'm a Southerner too," said the girl archly.

"I mean the disloyal traitors of the South—not the broad-minded patriots like your father," Suggs hastened to explain. "I say it's arrant nonsense this talk of such a parade by these traitors. I credit them with too much cunning to dare to flaunt their treason in the streets here to-night with a regiment of troops and the head of the Secret Service on the spot."

The little fellow expanded his chest and puffed his cheeks.

Billy doubled his fist, and made a dash for him.

With a suppressed scream, Mrs. Wilson caught him.

"Billy! for heaven's sake, are you crazy!"

They passed on down the street toward the Judge's house.

"I'm not so sure they will not parade, Mr. Suggs," Stella replied.

"Don't be alarmed, Miss Stella!" he urged soothingly. "I've taken ample means to protect you and your father from any attack of these assassins and desperadoes if they dare enter the town."

"I'm not afraid of them, Captain, she answered lightly.

"Of course not—we're here and ready for them. The very audacity of their manner is an insult to the Government."

"I like audacity. It stirs your blood," Stella cried, her brown eyes twinkling.

Suggs leaned nearer and said in his deepest voice:

"Let them dare this insult to authority to-night and you'll see audacity come to sudden grief in front of your father's house."

"Have you prepared an ambush?" Stella asked eagerly.

"Better. We've an extra hundred loyal policemen on the spot. Each of them is sworn to capture dead or alive any Ku Klux raider who shows his head. I hope they'll come—but it's too good to be true. With a dozen prisoners safe in jail, before to-morrow dawns I'll have the secrets of the Klan in my pocket. I'll make things hum

in Washington. Watch me. It's the big opportunity of life I've been waiting for—my only fear
is I'll miss it."

"I think you'll get it, Mr. Suggs," was the
laughing answer.

She had scarcely spoken, when a tow-headed
boy rushed into the middle of the street and
yelled,"

"Gee bucks! Look out! They're a comin'!"

Men, women and children rushed into the street.

Suggs stood irresolute and tightened his grip
on Stella's arm.

Down the street cheers burst forth and as they
died away the clatter of horses' hoofs rang clear,
distinct, defiant. They were riding slowly as in
dress parade.

Another cheer was heard and Suggs stepped
into the street and reconnoitred.

His face wore a puzzled look as he returned to
Stella's side.

"They've actually ridden past the regimental
camp. I can't understand why the Colonel did
not attack them."

"Gee Whilikens, there's a million of 'em!"
cried a boy nearby.

"Perhaps the Colonel thought discretion the
better part of valour, Mr. Suggs," suggested Stella
smilingly.

"Red tape," the detective explained with disgust— "he has no order. Just wait until the assassins walk into the trap I've laid for them. Come, we will hurry to your gate. I want you to see what happens."

They crossed the street and hurried to the Judge's place.

Suggs summoned the commander of his force of "metropolitan" police and in short sharp tones gave his orders.

"Are your men all ready, officer?"

"Yessir!"

"Fully armed?"

"You bet."

"Handcuffs ready?"

"All ready."

"Good. Throw your line, double column, across the street, stop the parade and arrest them one at a time."

Suggs squared his round shoulders as best he could; the officer saluted and returned to his place to execute the order.

When the cordon formed across the street the boys yelled and the news flashed from lip to lip far down the line. A great crowd quickly gathered surging back and forth in waves of excitement as the raiders approached.

The white ghostlike figures could now be seen,

the draped horse and rider appearing of gigantic size in the shimmering moonlight.

"Now we'll have some fun," exclaimed Suggs with a triumphant smile.

Stella trembled with excitement, two bright red spots appearing on her dimpled cheeks, her eyes sparkling.

Amid constant cheers from the crowds the line of white figures slowly approached the cordon of police without apparently noticing their existence.

"Now for the climax of the drama!" cried Suggs, watching with eager interest the rapidly closing space between the Clansmen and his police.

The officer in command, noting an uneasy tension along his lines, crossed the street in front of his men exhorting them.

"Stand your ground, boys!" he said firmly.

"Better save your hides, you scalawag skunks!" yelled an urchin from the crowd.

The leader of the Klan was now but ten feet away, towering tall, white and terrible, with an apparently interminable procession of mounted ghosts behind him.

The line of police swayed in the centre.

The Clansman leader lifted his hand, and the shrill scream of his whistle rang three times, and each white figure answered with a long piercing cry.

The police cordon broke into scurrying fragments and melted into the throngs on the sidewalks, while the procession of white and scarlet horsemen, without a pause, passed slowly on amid shouts of laughter from the people who had witnessed the fiasco.

"Well, I'll be d——! excuse me, Miss Stella!" Suggs cried in a stupor of blank amazement, his round little figure suddenly collapsing like a punctured balloon.

"You can't help admiring such men, Captain!" the girl laughed.

Suggs who had lost the power of speech wandered among the crowd in search of his commanding officer.

As the parade passed the Judge's gate, Stella stood wide-eyed, tense with excitement, watching the tall horseman with two scarlet crosses on his breast who led the procession.

"The spirit of some daring knight of the middle ages come back to earth again!" she cried. "Superb! Superb! I could surrender to such a man!"

A lace handkerchief fluttered from her bosom and waved a moment above her head. The tall figure turned in astonishment, bowed, tipped his spiked helmet, and without realising it suddenly reined his horse to a stand—and the whole line halted.

The leader whispered to a tall figure by his side, apparently his orderly, who turned to the line behind and shouted."

"Boys! three cheers for the little gal at the gate! She's all right! *The purtiest little gal in the countee—oh!*"

A rousing cheer rose from the ranks.

A ripple of sweet girlish laughter broke the silence which followed, the lace handkerchief fluttered again and the line moved slowly on.

Stella counted them.

"Only forty men. And they dared a regiment!" With another laugh, she deserted Suggs and disappeared in the flowers and shrubbery toward the house as the last echoes of the raiders died away in the distance.

The Clansmen descended a hill, turned sharply to the right toward the river and broke into a quick gallop. Within thirty minutes they entered a forest on the river bank, and down its dim aisles, lit by moonbeams, slowly wound their way to their old rendezvous.

The signal was given to dismount and disrobe the horses. Within a minute the white figures gathered about a newly opened grave.

The men began to whisper excitedly to one another.

"What's this?"

"What's the matter?"

"Who's dead?"

"You're too many for me!"

"What's up, Steve Hoyle?" asked one of the raiders.

"It's beyond me, sonny. The Grand Dragon of the State honours us with his presence to-night and is in command—he will no doubt explain. Have a drink." He handed the group a flask of whiskey, and passed on.

When the men had assembled beside the shallow grave, the chaplain led in prayer.

The tall figure with the double scarlet cross on his breast removed his helmet and faced the men.

"Boys," began John Graham, "you have assembled here to-night for the last time as members of the Invisible Empire!"

"Hell!"

"What's that?"

The exclamations, half incredulous, half angry, came from every direction with suddenness and unanimity which showed the men to be utterly unprepared for such an announcement.

"Yes," the even voice went on, "I hold in my hand an official order of the Grand Wizard of the

Empire, dissolving its existence for all time. Our
Commander-in-chief has given the word. As
loyal members of the order, we accept his message."

"Then our parade to-night was not a defiance
of these soldiers who have marched into town?"
sneered a voice.

"No, Steve Hoyle, it was not. Our parade
to-night was in accordance with this order of
dissolution. It was our last formal appearance.
Our work is done——"

Steve saw in a flash his opportunity to defeat
his enemy and make himself not only the master
of his Congressional District but of the state itself.

"Not by a damn sight!" snapped the big square
jaw.

"You refuse as the commander of this district
to obey the order of the Grand Wizard?" asked
the tall quiet figure.

"I refuse, John Graham, to accept your word
as the edict of God!" was the quick retort. "Our
men can vote on this and decide for themselves."

"Yes, vote on it!"

"We'll decide for ourselves!"

The quick responses which came from all sides
showed the temper of the men. John Graham
stepped in front of the big leader of the district.

"Look here, Steve Hoyle, I want no trouble
with you to-night, nor in the future—but I'm

"Some of the men were sobbing"

going to carry this order into execution here and now."

"Let's see you do it!" was the defiant answer.

"I will," he continued. "Boys!"

There was the ring of conscious authority in his tones and the men responded with sharp attention.

"You have each sworn to obey your superior officer on the penalty of your life?"

"Yes!"

"You are men of your word. As the Grand Dragon of the State I command you to deliver to me immediately your helmets and robes."

With the precision of soldiers they deposited them in the open grave. Steve Hoyle surrendered his last.

When all had been placed in the grave, John Graham removed his own, reverently placed it with the others, tied two pieces of pine into the form of the fiery cross, lighted its ends, drew the ritual of the Klan from his pocket, set it on fire and held it over the grave while the ashes slowly fell on the folds of the white and scarlet regalia which he also ignited. Some of the men were sobbing. While the regalia rapidly burned he turned and said:

"Boys, I thank you. You have helped me do a painful thing. But it is best. Our work is done. We have rescued our state from Negro rule. We dissolve this powerful secret order in time to save you from persecution, exile, imprisonment and death. The National Government is getting ready to strike. When the blow falls it will be on the vanished shadow of a ghost. There's a time to fight, and a time to retreat. We retreat from a field of victory.

"I should have dissolved the Klan a month ago. I confess to you a secret. I waited because I meant to strike with it a blow at a personal enemy. I realise now that I stood as your leader on the brink of the precipice of social anarchy. Forgive me for the wrong I might have done, had you followed me. As Grand Dragon of the Empire I declare this order dissolved forever in the state of North Carolina!"

He seized a shovel and covered with earth and leaves the ashes of the burned regalia.

Steve Hoyle stepped quickly in front of his rival. The veins on his massive neck stood out like cords and his eyes shone ominously in the moonlight. The slender figure of John Graham instinctively stiffened at the threat of his movement as the two men faced each other.

"The Klan is now a thing of the past?" asked Steve.

"Yes."

"As though it had never been?"

"As though it had never existed."

"Then your authority is at an end?"

"As an officer of the Klan, yes. As a leader of men, no."

"The officer only interests me—Boys!" Steve's angry voice rang with defiance.

The men gathered closer.

"The Invisible Empire is no more. Its officers are as dead as the ashes of its ritual. Meet me here to-morrow night at eleven o'clock to organise a new order of patriots! Will you come?"

"Yes!"

"You bet your life!"

The answers seemed to leap from every throat at the same moment.

John Graham's face went white for a moment and his fist closed.

"Patriotism is the last refuge of a scoundrel, Steve Hoyle," he said with slow emphasis.

"And traitors pose as moral leaders," was the retort.

"Time will show which of us is a traitor. Will you dare thus to defy me and reorganise this Klan?"

"Wait and see!"

John Graham stepped close to his rival, and, in a low voice unheard save by the man to whom he spoke, said:

"Take back that order and tell those men to go home and stay there."

"I'll see you in hell first!" came the answer in a growl.

Scarcely had the words passed his lips when John Graham's fist shot into his rival's face.

The blow was delivered so quickly Steve's heavy form struck the ground before the astonished men could interfere.

In a moment a dozen men sprang between them and John said with quiet emphasis, glaring at his enemy:

"I'll be in my office at ten o'clock to-morrow morning, to receive any communication you may wish to make—you understand!"

And deliberately mounting his horse, he rode away into the night alone.

CHAPTER IV

THE OLD CODE

JOHN GRAHAM walked briskly to his office
the next morning at a quarter to ten, and found
Dan Wiley standing at the door.

The lank mountaineer merely nodded, followed
the young lawyer into the office, and stood in
silence watching him as he opened a case of duelling
pistols which had been handed down through
four generations of his family.

"Don't do it," said Dan abruptly.

"I've got to."

"Ain't no sense in it."

"It's the only way, Dan, and I'm going to ask
you to be my second."

Dan placed his big rough hand on the younger
man's shoulders.

"Lemme be fust, not second."

"It's not my way!"

"That's why I'm axin ye. You're the biggest
man in the state! I seed it last night as ye stood
there makin' that speech to the boys. You'll
be the Governor if ye don't do some fool thing
like this. If ye fight 'im, an' he kills ye, your'e a

goner. If you kill him, you're ruined—what's the use?"

"It can't be helped," was the quiet answer.

"Are ye goin' ter kill 'im?"

"Yes. The Klan was the only way to save our civilisation. I've sowed the wind and now I begin to see that somebody must reap the whirlwind. I realised it all in a flash last night when that scoundrel called the men to reorganise."

"They won't follow him."

"The fools will, and there are thousands outside clamouring to get in. I've kept the young and reckless out as far as possible. Steve Hoyle knows that he can beat me for Congress with this new wildcat Klan at his back. He hasn't sense enough to see that the spell of authority once broken, he wields a power no human hand can control. It will be faction against faction, neighbour against neighbour, man against man—the end martial law, prison bars and the shadow of the gallows. I can save the lives of thousands of men, and my state from crime and disgrace by killing this fool as I'd kill a mad dog, and I'm going to do it!"

"Hit'll ruin ye, boy!"

"I know it."

"Look here, John Graham, do me a special favour. Leave Steve to me. My wife's dead and I aint got a chick or a child—you've defended me without a cent and you're the best friend I've got in the world. It's my turn now. Nobody would miss me."

"I'd miss you, Dan!" said John slowly.

The two men silently clasped hands and looked into each other's faces.

"You're a fool to do this, boy"—the mountaineer's voice broke.

"Of course, Dan, many of our old-fashioned ways are foolish but at least they hold the honour of man, and the virtue of woman dearer than human life!"

A boy suddenly opened the door without knocking and handed John a note.

He read it aloud with a scowl:

My friends have decided that I shall not play into your hands by an absurd appeal to the Code of the Dark Ages. I'll fight you in my own way at a time and place of my own choosing and with weapons that will be effective.

STEVE HOYLE.

"Now, by gum, you'll have to leave 'im to me," laughed the mountaineer.

John tore the note into bits and turned to the boy:

"No answer, you can go."

"He'll pick you off some night from behind a tree," warned Dan.

"Sneak and coward!" muttered John.

"Ye won't let me help ye?"

"No, go home and disband your men."

"May they keep the rig?"

"If you won't go on a raid."

"I'll not, unless you need me, John Graham," cried the mountaineer grasping again his young leader's hand.

"All right. I can trust you. Keep their costumes in your house under lock and key until I call for them."

As Dan turned slowly through the door he drawled over his shoulder: "You'll need 'em purty quick!"

CHAPTER V

WHEN Dan Wiley closed the door John turned to his desk and drew from a pigeon hole the mass of legal papers containing the evidence he had gathered of Butler's theft of his estate.

The dissolution of the Klan had left him only the process of the law by which to recover it. Yet it was only a question of time when the decision of the Supreme Court would hurl the Judge from the Graham home and arraign him for impeachment.

Now that he was ready to file the suit, his mind was in a tumult of hesitation. The soft invisible hand of a girl was holding his hand. He gazed steadily at the documents and saw nothing that was within. The ink lines slowly resolved themselves into the raven glossy hair of Stella piled in curling confusion above her white forehead, and he was trying in vain to find the depths of her wonderful eyes.

Something in the expression of those eyes held his memory in a perpetual spell — their remarkable size and their dilation when she spoke. They seemed to enfold him in a soft mantle of light.

He suddenly bundled the papers, replaced them, and took up his pen.

"I've got to see her—that's all!" he exclaimed. "Who knows? Perhaps I'm answering the great summons of life. I'll put it to the test. At least I'll not throw my chance away for a house, some trees and a few acres of dirt. When Love calls life's too short for revenge."

On a sheet of delicate old note paper with a crest of yellow and black at the top, he wrote:

My Dear Miss Butler:

You were gracious enough to ask me to call again. I cannot believe your words were mere conventional phrases. Their accent was too genuine and sincere. So I beg the privilege of calling to-day while your father, my valiant political enemy, is busy down town with the delegates to his convention which meets to-morrow. I anxiously await your answer.

Sincerely,

John Graham.

"Unless I've mistaken her character, she'll see me!" he mused as he sealed the note.

He went at once to Mrs. Wilson's, found Alfred, and gave him the missive.

"Take that to the Judge's and give it to Miss Stella."

Alfred stared.

"Down to de ole place!"

"Yes, of course."

Alfred sat down and laughed.

"Well, fore de Lawd, doan dat beat ye!"

"Shut up, and hurry back—I'll wait for you at the office."

"Yassah, right away, sah!"

"And Alfred, not a word to a living soul of this."

"No, sah, cose not Marse John—I know how tis 'my sef'—de course er true love ain't run smooth wid me nuther."

"Quick, now, don't you lose a minute."

John returned to his office to await with impatience the word that would mean the beginning of a new chapter in his life.

Alfred placed the note carefully under his hat and hastened to the Judge's, laughing and chuckling to himself.

For reasons best known to himself he entered by the carriage way.

At the wide double gate still stood the old lodge-keeper's cottage, a relic of the slave régime. In the cottage Aunt Julie Ann lived with Uncle Isaac, her latest husband. Alfred had once been honoured with that relationship before the war, but Isaac had whipped him and taken Aunt Julie Ann by force of arms.

Alfred was much the larger man of the two, tall, awkward and slow of movement, while Isaac was small and active as a cat. The agility of his movements had swept Aunt Julie Ann's imagination by storm. The contrast to her own three hundred pounds had no doubt been the secret charm.

She had loudly professed her love for Alfred until she saw Isaac thrash him, and without a word she surrendered to the new lord and refused to recognise her former husband.

This happened two years before the war and Alfred had watched and waited the day of his revenge to dawn. Many a night he had prowled around her cottage spying and listening at the keyhole for her cry of help. He had heard at last that Isaac was beating her unmercifully and he chuckled with grim satisfaction. Every opportunity he got he hung around the cottage and listened for the long expected cry. As he approached the gates this morning in a peculiarly romantic frame of mind, remembering the mission he was on, he heard Uncle Isaac's voice in sharp accents within, hectoring it over his former spouse.

He crept to the door and listened breathlessly.

"Dar now, I'se jes' in time ter sabe my lady love!"

He peeped cautiously through the keyhole and saw Aunt Julie Ann's huge form busy at the ironing board, while Isaac sat majestically in a rocker delivering to her an eloquent discourse on Sanctification in general and his own sinless perfection in particular. Isaac had changed his name several times after the war, following the example of many Negroes who were afraid the use of their old master's name might some day serve as the badge of slavery. He had lately become a Northern Methodist exhorter of great fame and went from church to church holding revivals, particularly among the sisters of the church, calling them to the life of stainless purity of those who had not merely "salvation," as the ordinary Methodist or Baptist understood it, but "sanctification" as only those of the inner circle of the Lord knew it.

Isaac had long ago been "sanctified," and had declared not only his sinless nature but had boldy proclaimed himself a prophet of the new dispensation and had finally fixed his name as "Isaac the Apostle," which had been simplified by busy clerks in written form to Isaac A. Postle.

Aunt Julie Ann had heard of his wonderful success in his sanctification meetings with misgivings, as the large majority of his converts were invariably among the sisters. She had finally

dared to question the authenticity of his apostolic
call. Her scepticism had aroused Isaac to a
frenzy of religious enthusiasm. That the wife
of his bosom should be the only voice to question
his divine mission was proof positive that she had
in some mysterious way become possessed of the
devil—perhaps seven devils.

He determined to cast them out—by moral
suasion if possible—if not, by the main strength
of his good right arm. He must set his own
house in order lest the very source of his inspiration
be poisoned by lack of faith. He was devoting
this morning to the task when Alfred arrived.

He had just finished a long and fervid explanation of the mystery of Sanctification.

"Fur de las' time I axes ye, 'oman, what sez
ye ter de word er de Lawd?"

Aunt Julie Ann banged the board with the iron
and merely grunted:

"Huh!"

Isaac rose and repeated his question with rising
wrath:

"What sez ye ter de word er de Lawd?"

"I ain' heared de Lawd say nuttin yit!"

"An' why ain't ye?"

"Case you keep so much fuss I can't hear
nuttin', Isaac Graham!"

"Doan you call me dat name, you brazen sinner

dat sets in de seat er de scornful! Is ye ready ter repent an' sin no mo?"

Isaac approached her threateningly and Alfred, watching with bulging eyes, clutched the stick he had picked up.

"Tech me if ye dare—I bus' yo head open wid dis flat-iron!"

Isaac knew his duty now and determined to perform it without further ceremony. The anointed of the Lord had been threatened by the ungodly. He drew a seasoned hickory withe from a crack where he had hidden it and approached his sceptical spouse.

Aunt Julie Ann began to whimper.

"Put down dat flat-iron!" he sternly commanded.

Alfred peering through the keyhole gasped in amazement as he saw her drop the iron heavily on the floor.

Isaac raised his switch and began to whip her. Around and around she flew screaming, begging, pleading for mercy. But Isaac continued to lay on steadily.

Alfred tried to rise and rush to the rescue but somehow he couldn't move. To his own surprise the performance fascinated him. He sat peering with satisfaction.

"Dat's paying her back now fur leavin' me fer

dat low live rascal. Give it to her, old man! Give it to her! She sho' deserves it!"

At length Isaac paused, and eyed her steadily while he shook his switch with unction.

"I axes ye now, does ye believe in de Sanctification er de Saints?"

"Yes, Lawd, I sees it now!" she cried with fervour.

"An' thanks me fer showin' ye de error er yo' way?"

"Yes, honey! I'm gwine ter seek dat Sanctification myself!"

"Glory! We'se er comin' on!"

Aunt Julie Ann picked up the flat-iron. Isaac eyed her with suspicion but he was too much elated with his victory to notice anything unusual in her manner.

"Ye b'lieves now in de Sanctification er de Lawd's messenger Isaac A. Postle?"

With a sudden flash of her eye Aunt Julie Ann hurled the flat-iron straight at the head of the Lord's messenger saying:

"No, I ain't sed dat yit!"

But Isaac was quick. He dodged in time. The corner of the flat-iron merely tipped his ear and smashed through the window.

He grabbed his ear with sudden pain and gripped his switch with renewed zeal.

"I see I'se des begun—one debble out, but dey's six mo' ter come!"

Again he whipped her around the room, threw her down, held her hair and banged her head against the floor.

"Fur de las' time I axes ye, is de Lawd's messenger, Isaac A. Postle, a sanctified one?"

Bang! Bang! Bang! went her head against the planks.

"Yes honey, I sees it now!" she cried with enthusiasm.

"Dat's de way!"

"Does ye lub me fur showin' ye de light?"

Bang! Bang! went her head.

"Yes, Lawd, I lub ye."

"Say it strong."

Bang! Bang! went her head.

"I lubs ye, my honey, yes I do!" shouted Aunt Julie Ann.

"An' I'se de only man dat ye ebber lub?"

A moment's pause, and again bang! bang! went her head.

Alfred couldn't wait for the answer; he gripped his stick, sprang through the door, knocked the Apostle flat on his back, and jumped on him.

Aunt Julie Ann was more astonished than Isaac at her sudden deliverance.

She scrambled to her feet and gazed for a moment

in amazement at Alfred as he pummelled Isaac's head against the floor with one hand and pounded him with the other.

At every thump of his head Isaac yelled:

"God sabe me! de debble done got me! Help, Lawd, help! Save me Lawd—save me now!"

Alfred pounded steadily away.

Aunt Julie Ann, when she caught her breath, grasped Alfred's arm and yelled:

"What yer doin' here, nigger!"

He wrenched his arm loose from her grasp and hit Isaac a smashing blow in the mouth as he cried again for help.

"Git offen my ole man. I tell ye!" screamed Aunt Julie Ann, gripping Alfred by the throat.

"Name er God, 'oman, what yer doin' when I comes here ter save ye!" cried Alfred, wrenching himself from her grip and returning to his work on Isaac.

"Git offen 'im, I tell ye, fo' I bus' yer open!" she panted, towering above the writhing pair. She began to pound Alfred over the head with her fists, but he worked steadily away on Isaac without noticing the interruptions.

Suddenly Aunt Julie Ann threw both arms around his neck, bent his lank figure double across Isaac's prostrate form, and hurled her three hundred pounds squarely across the two writhing men. There was dead silence for a moment and then Isaac groaned:

"God save me now! we'se bof gone! De house done fall on us!"

"Na! honey, it's me!" cried Aunt Julie Ann, "an' I got 'im in de gills!"

She rolled over and pulled Alfred with her—both hands gripped to his throat.

In a moment Isaac was on his feet.

"De Lawd hear my cry!" he exclaimed with unction, pouncing on Alfred and pounding him unmercifully while his faithful spouse held him fast. Alfred found his voice at last, and began to yell murder.

Steve Hoyle, who was pacing the walk in front of the Judge's anxiously waiting an answer to a pleading letter he had sent to Stella asking for an interview, heard the cries and rushed to Alfred's rescue.

He pulled Isaac and Aunt Julie Ann off in time to save his hat and portions of his clothes.

As he entered the cottage, he had seen instantly the note in John Graham's handwriting which Alfred had dropped on the floor. He picked it up hastily and put it in his pocket.

When Alfred got out the door, he did not stand on the order of his going. He struck a bee

line for John Graham's office and ran every step
of the way without looking back.

John was pacing the floor, his heart beating
out the interminable minutes.

Alfred burst into the room, his nose bleeding,
a gash across his forehead, his clothes torn and
spotted with the blood from his nose. He was
still wild with the fear of death which had clutched
his soul as the light of day faded under Aunt
Julie Ann's awful grip on his throat.

He dropped, panting and speechless, on the floor.

"For God's sake, Alfred, what's happened!"
John cried, seizing a glass of water and pressing
it to his lips.

"Dey kill me, Marse John!"

"Who did it?—what for?"

"De folks at de Judge's."

"Where's my note?"

"Dunno sah!"

"Didn't you deliver it?"

"Dunno sah!"

"Did you go to the house?"

"Dunno sah!"

"Where did this happen?"

"At de gate, sah, dey wuz layin' fer me—De
Judge mus' er tole 'em ter kill me."

"Who did it?"

"Ole Isaac and Julie Ann jump on me fust,

but tow'd de last dey wuz er dozen. Six un 'em
wuz er beatin' me on de head at de same time,
three er four wuz er settin' on top er me, two had
me by the throat an' de res' un 'em wuz er steady
kickin' me in de stummick. Dey'd er had me sho'
by dis time ef I hadn't kotch my breaf an' holler'd."

"And who helped you?"

"Mr. Steve Hoyle wuz dar ter see Miss Stella
an' he run in an' pulled 'em off." When I lit
out for home I wuz er sight sho nuff. I hear Miss
Stella come up ter Mr. Steve an' bust out laffin'
fit ter kill herself."

"And you don't know what became of the note?"

"Yassah! cose sah! dey tuck hit away fum me
and tore it up—dat's what I fit 'em 'bout—yassah!"

John's face was white with rage. He sent
Alfred home, sat down at his desk, and drew out
the papers he had laid aside. The Judge had
won. He had covered him with infamy in the
eyes of his beautiful daughter and had dared to
perpetrate this infamous outrage. He couldn't
understand Aunt Julie Ann's part in the row, but
the evidence of Alfred's plight could not be
mistaken.

For three hours with stern set face he worked
completing the case of Graham vs. Butler. At
four o'clock he had entered the suit and an officer
served the papers on the astonished Judge.

CHAPTER VI

SCALAWAG AND CARPETBAGGER

JOHN GRAHAM, as leader of the opposition, as well as for personal reasons, was early on the grounds with half a dozen trusted lieutenants to watch the action of the Republican County Convention. He was curious to observe the effects of his suit on the Judge and his followers. He soon discovered that the scathing recital of fraud which he had incorporated into the form of his complaint as published in the morning's paper was a mistake. It had been accepted by the mottled crew of nondescript politicians and Negroes as proof positive of his own depravity and the Judge's spotless purity.

The Convention was seated in the open air on improvised boards. The Judge was peculiarly sensitive to the atmosphere of a crowd of Negroes. He had to associate with them to get their votes, but like all poor white men of Southern birth, he hated them without measure.

This Convention of his home county was the most important crisis in the development of his ambitions as the leader of his party in the South.

He was a candidate for the United States Senate. Delegates were to be elected to-day to the state convention. Unless he could go with a united front from his home county he was doomed.

His opponent, Alexander Larkin, was the boldest, most unscrupulous, and powerful Carpet-bag adventurer who had ever entered the South from the slums of the North.

Larkin had made himself the Chairman of the Republican State Executive Committee, and was running neck and neck with the Judge for the Senate. He had determined to break his opponent's backbone by capturing the whole, or at least a part of the delegates from Butler's home county. The audacity of this movement had fairly taken the Judge's breath. He halted Suggs in his thrilling pursuit of Ku Klux evidence and sent him North on an important mission. He meant to be fully prepared for any trick Larkin might spring. Suggs was bustling about among the delegates conscious that he was the trusted lieutenant of the coming man.

The Carpetbagger had so timed his anony-mous letter to John Graham that the shadow of disgrace thus thrown over Butler's name would give him the balance of power. He could not foresee the chain of trivial events which would produce the terrific document John Graham had filed. Every word of its passionate arraignment had the sting of a scorpion, and its effects had been electrical. By instinct the crowd had accepted John's suit as a blow at the cause and Butler had become their champion.

As the Judge approached the crowd accompanied by Stella and Steve Hoyle, John saw with sinking heart that the first effect of his suit had been to bring Steve and Stella closer together and to dig an impassable gulf between him and the girl he had begun unconsciously to worship. She had evidently laid aside her hatred of politics and become her father's champion. And he knew that Steve Hoyle had lost no time in this crisis in poisoning her mind forever against him. In fact Steve had spent the morning by her side developing the bitter sentences in his complaint into revelations of hereditary insanity and envenomed malice.

The girl had, however, taken his statements with reservations. She would stand by her father before the world and she would publicly insult John Graham if he ever dared give her the opportunity, but deep down in her heart she half suspected the truth. The memory of the bitter feud between her mother and father over some secret connected with this estate and her father's shuffling evasions, returned to her now with startling import.

Her mother was of the old régime of the South, an aristocrat of aristocrats to her finger tips. Her people had blotted her very name from their memory for her marriage to Butler. She had fiercely resented to the day of her death this ostracism. The fear that her husband was a scoundrel, which slowly grew into a certainty in later years, at last broke her proud spirit. She gave up the struggle and died.

There were moments in which Stella felt this inherited repugnance to her father when the proud spirit of her mother's blood ruled in her soul. There were other moments when she felt the necessity of tricks and lies to make life agreeable and accepted her father as of the inevitable order of human existence.

This morning she was her father's daughter. Whether he was guilty or innocent she would show John Graham and his proud Bourbon set her contempt for them and their opinions.

As the three reached the edge of the crowd she was smiling graciously on Steve in answer to a sally of his cheap wit. She fixed John with a look of contempt and his soul grew sick with the consciousness that he had paid too great a price for his suit against the Judge. In her anger she was superb. The very air about her seemed charged with the intensity of her personality. She radiated it in every direction. It was the consciousness of this intensity of nature which drew John to her with resistless power. No other type of woman could interest him, and Stella was endowed with this subtle magnetism as no human being he had ever met. It spoke in every movement of her body, in every accent of her voice.

As she passed and turned her back on him, the sense of a hopeless and irreparable loss crushed his spirit. The words of the preacher rang in his soul, "What shall it profit a man if he gain the whole world and forfeit his life. "

"What are houses and lands after all, before the elemental forces which make life worth while," he muttered. "I've an almost irresistible impulse to knock Steve Hoyle down, seize her in my arms, smother her with kisses and carry her off to some cave on a mountain! To the devil with goods and chattels, houses and lands."

With a start he came down from the clouds of fancy. She had dismissed Steve, taken the Judge's arm, and was actually going to walk down the aisle through that mob of Negroes and greasy politicians and accompany him to the platform.

When they reached the centre of the crowd, seated in semicircle about the covered speaker's stand, pandemonium broke loose. The Judge received the most remarkable ovation of his life.

The throng leaped to their feet and screamed themselves horse.

"Keep your house Judge!" yelled a henchman. "Houses were built for patriots, and jails for traitors!"

The Judge bowed and again the crowd yelled.

Larkin from the platform watched the demonstration with amazement.

"I've miscalculated. They're all thieves and scoundrels. I've made him a hero."

With a hypocritical smile he seized the Judge's hand, wrung it heartily, congratulated him, and drew him to the platform. Stella sprang lightly up after him, took a rosebud from her belt, pinned it on her father's slouchy ill-fitting broadcloth coat, kissed him and amid the cheers of the mob retraced her steps and left the ground with Steve Hoyle.

John watched her lift her parasol above her dainty head with smothered curses at his folly. He had unconsciously taken his own hat off and stood bareheaded in the broiling Southern sun of a June day. The bitterness of his mistake stirred him to more dogged persistence. With an effort he turned to the Judge and the Convention—trying in vain to shake off the impression Stella had left. But he found his mind constantly wandering from the scene. Wherever he looked,

within or without, he saw the delicate oval face
with those great brown eyes smiling as they did
the night he met her in the hall of his old home.

At length he awoke from his reverie with his
eye resting unconsciously on Larkin, the Judge's
opponent. He had never seen him before, though
his name had become known in every county
of the state.

He was a man of more than the average height,
of powerful build, high intellectual forehead, a
full beard, long, silken, snow white. His hair,
also long and white, was inclined to curl at the ends,
and a pair of piercing black eyes looked out fear-
lessly from shaggy brows. He carried himself
with instinctive dignity, and his whole appearance
proclaimed a bold and powerful leader of men.

Rumour said that he had been a Wesleyan
preacher in England but had been expelled in some
factional fight and had sought his fortunes in
America. Darker rumour whispered that he had
a criminal record and that he had never even
attained citizenship in the country of his adoption.
Such rumours, however, counted for nothing in the
tainted atmosphere of the riot and revolution of
the Reconstruction period. From the sewers of
the North, jail birds and ex-convicts had poured
into the stricken South as vultures follow the wake
of a victorious army.

In two years Larkin had proven himself a party leader of remarkable executive ability and on the hustings had shown himself an orator of undoubted eloquence. He was fast becoming the idol of the more daring and radical wing of his party. He boldly proclaimed and practiced Negro equality and held up to public scorn any man who dared to quibble on the issue.

So bold and radical were his utterances the Negroes were a little afraid of him. Yet he was steadily gaining in his influence over them. He knew that they constituted nine-tenths of the voting strength of the Republican party in the South, and that ultimately the man who pandered most skilfully to their passions must become master of the situation.

He had laid siege to Uncle Isaac immediately on his arrival and had played on his vanity so deftly that the Apostle of Sanctification had been completely fascinated by the Carpetbagger.

The moment Larkin's eye rested on Isaac seated in the crowd he saw in a flash the master stroke by which he could break the spell of the Judge's influence over the delegates. He quickly threaded his way to the Apostle's side and escorted him to the speakers' stand with his arm around his waist. He lifted him to the platform, forced the Judge to rise and shake hands, and seated Isaac by

Butler's side. The Negroes burst into a frenzy of applause.

So elated was Isaac by his newly found honours he began to interrupt the meeting by fervid religious exclamations to the intense disgust of the Judge who squirmed with increasing anger at each new outburst. When Isaac recognised any of his dusky acquaintances in the crowd he waved his hand and pointed his remarks in that direction.

"Yas Lawd! De year er juberlee is come, an' I'se right here!"

A loud guffaw would invariably answer his sally.

Larkin ostentatiously consulted Isaac from time to time as to the conduct of the convention and every Negro watched him spellbound.

The Judge's henchmen were dismayed at the impending stampede by the Carpetbagger. Butler had assured them the night before that they had nothing to fear from Larkin. But it was only too apparent that he had underestimated his opponent. Larkin's commanding appearance, his magnetism and eloquence, the boldness and evident sincerity of his profession of Negro equality were steadily winning adherents.

Personally the Judge cut a poor figure beside him with his slouchy ill-fitting clothes, his fawning shuffling walk, his drooping head, shifting eyes, and his vague professions of platitudes.

Butler watched Larkin's sudden growth of power with sullen rage. He had in reserve a weapon which he had found in the Carpetbagger's English career, with which he could crush him at a single blow, but he had not expected to be forced to the extreme necessity of using it. For many reasons he wished to beat Larkin in an open fight. The weapon he could use was a dangerous one. He knew that Larkin had learned the facts concerning his confiscation of the Graham estate, and he was not sure how far his resentment would go in retaliation for an attack on his personal character. But he determined to put a stop to Isaac's insolence which was rapidly becoming unendurable.

The Judge leaned over toward the enthusiastic Apostle and with a frown said:

"Shut your mouth and behave yourself!"

Isaac subsided with a look of injured innocence directed in mute appeal toward Larkin.

Again the Carpetbagger saw his opportunity. He approached Isaac, seized his hand, slipped his arm around his shoulder and whispered:

"Brother, I'm going to make a motion to amend the Judge's list of delegates by substituting six men of colour for six of the poor white men he has chosen. I'll put your name first. Will you make a speech in favour of my motion?"

"Dat I will!"

"Then repeat that story of the vision you told me last night, and apply it to the Judge—will you do it?"

"Make de movement, an' I sho' ye!" whispered Isaac.

Larkin's bold motion, a direct appeal to the Negro to use his power against the white man, took the Judge's breath. He stared at his opponent in blank amazement while Larkin smiled at him with good-natured contempt.

"And I have asked," continued the Carpet-bagger, "a distinguished leader of his race, Mr. Isaac A. Postle, a constituent and neighbour of Judge Butler, to address the Convention before the motion is opened to general debate. I am sure the Convention will give its unanimous consent to hear him."

The roar of applause which greeted this remark left no doubt as to their consent. Larkin seized Isaac and drew him before the speaker's table with his arm again affectionately around him.

Isaac was in a broad grin and evidently enjoyed his honours. He cleared his throat and glanced at the Judge. The Negroes burst into roars of laughter and the Apostle lifted his hand solemnly for silence.

Butler scowled and shuffled uneasily while Larkin's face was wreathed in smiles.

"Gemmens an' feller citizens!" Isaac began with great deliberation. "I'se called by de Lawd dis mawnin' ter come up on high and expose de vision dat I seed in de dead er de night las' week. I drempt a dream. I dream dat I die and go ter heaben. An' as I wuz gwine long up de hill ter de pearly gates who should I meet comin' down de hill but our good frien' Judge Butler——"

The Judge gave a sharp little angry cough, pulled his long black whiskers and crossed his legs quickly. Isaac glanced at him and walled his eyes at the dusky crowd who broke into another roar of laughter.

"Yassah!" he went on, "I met Judge Butler comin' down de hill lookin' pow'ful sad. An' he say ter me:

"'Isaac, whar ye gwine?'

"'Gwine ter heben,' sezzi.

"'Ye can't git in!' sezze.

"'Why so?' sezzi.

"'Case ye got ter be er ridin',' sezze—'I jes come down frum dar—an' hits des lak I tell ye!'

"'Is dat so?' sezzi.

"'But I tell ye what we kin do, Isaac!' sezze.

"'I'll git on yo back an' ride up to de gate, an' we bof git in.'"

"Dat seem all right ter me fust off so I hump mysef an' de Jedge git on my back, an' I gallup

up de hill ter de pearly gates, an' de angel Gabul,
he look over de fence an' say:

"'Who's dar?'

"'Hit's me, Jedge Butler,' sezze.

"'Ridin' er walkin'?' de angel say.

"'Er ridin'!' sezze.

An' I chuckled ter myse'f dat I'se er settin my
feet in de gates er glory!

An' den de angel say:

"'Des hitch yer hoss outside an' come in!'

"An' bress God! ef de Jedge didn't hitch me ter
de pos' on de outside an' go in an' leave
me dar!"

Again th crowd screamed with laughter.
Wave after wave swept them while Isaac folded
his hands across his little protruding stomach
and laughed with them. In vain the chairman
rapped for order.

The Judge flushed red with anger and called
Suggs to his side. Larkin bent low his face
between his hands, convulsed with laughter.

When at length the tumult wore itself out Isaac's
voice rang over the assembly in sharp vibrant
triumphant tones:

"An' I moves yer, sah, dat we all unanimously
second de motion er Brer Larkin!"

Amid a shout of approval he sat down.

The Carpetbagger, elated by his success,

determined to make a bold_r stroke, capture the entire delegation and put the Judge out of the race.

He leaped to his feet and launched at once into
an eloquent appeal for the equal rights of man,
meaning, of course, the right of the Negro race to
rule the white man of the South, the former slave
to rule his master. Bold as a lion by instinct,
he did not quibble over words. He told the Negro
that his hour had come to strike for his right by
force of arms if need be. He denounced the Ku
Klux Klan in the bitterest terms. Every Negro
followed his scathing words with breathless attention. For the moment he was the veritable prophet of the Most High God. N ver before had
they heard any man in public dare thus to arraign
this dreaded order of white and scarlet horsemen.
Here was their champion whose valiant soul knew
not the fear of man, ghost, clansman or devil.
He was transfigured before th ir yes into the
white-haired prophet of the Lord, and they hung
on his every word as inspired.

In another moment he would have made his
motion for a solid Negro delegation and stampeded
the Convention had it not been for the single burst
of eloquence with which he closed his speech.
Just at the moment when he held every heart in
the dusky host in the hollow of his hand, he
thundered:

"Against the white traitor of the South who has perpetrated these wrongs on your defenseless heads I hurl the everlasting curse of God! Only a race of dastards and cowards would thus sneak under the cover of night to strike their foes!"

He had scarcely uttered the words when Billy Graham rushed from the outer circle of the crowd where he had sauntered with Mrs. Wilson, surrounded by a dozen fun-making youngsters, and ran toward the platform.

"Wait a minute!" he said, with uplifted hand, his voice quivering with rage.

Larkin's arm dropped; he halted in amazement, every eye fixed on Billy. John Graham sprang to his feet with a muttered oath of surprise in time to see Billy square himself in front of the speaker and say:

"If you think the Southern people a race of cowards and dastards come down off that platform and knock this chip off my shoulder, you old white-livered cur!"

He placed a chip on his shoulder and strutted before Larkin. The Carpetbagger was too astonished to reply. He gazed at the boy in confusion and muttered an inarticulate protest.

Billy jumped on the platform and walked around him like a game bantam, crying:

"Knock it off—d——you! knock it off! If

you want to test it! A dozen of my friends are out there, yours all around you, a hundred to one, but knock it off! knock it off!"

John Graham had reached the platform by this time, seized Billy and led him back through the crowd to Mrs. Wilson who was in hysterics, the boys vainly trying to quiet her.

"What the devil's the matter with you—have you gone crazy?" John whispered, shaking Billy fiercely. "Go home and behave yourself!"

"Attend to your own business, John Graham; I'm attending to mine!" was Billy's sullen answer. And without another word he led Mrs. Wilson away followed by his companions, while John gazed after him with increasing astonishment.

In the confusion which followed Billy's sudden challenge the Judge saw his chance. He sprang to his feet and moved to adjourn for dinner. Before Larkin could recover himself the motion was carried and the Convention adjourned.

Butler turned to the Carpetbagger and said:

"I wish to see you in my hotel immediately on a matter of the gravest importance."

"I haven't time, Judge," Larkin carelessly answered.

"I'm in no mood to be trifled with," answered the Judge.

"It's a waste of time, your Honour—you're

a back number. Why should I talk with you?"

"There's one reason big enough to interest you," the Judge answered with sinister suggestion.

Larkin fixed his opponent a moment with his piercing eyes and said with contempt:

"I'll join you in a moment."

The Judge beckoned to Suggs who had hovered near, and the detective handed him a package of documents from his inside pocket. The movement was not lost on Larkin who was watching his enemy with uneasiness.

Suggs accompanied the Judge to his room at the hotel and awaited his call outside the door. Larkin looked at him with a scowl as he entered.

The Judge adjusted his slouchy coat, shuffled his feet, and stroked his beard with deliberation as Larkin seated himself.

"I'm going to ask you, Larkin," he began, "to write out your resignation as Chairman of our State Executive Committee and withdraw from this race."

The Carpetbagger laughed aloud.

"Well, you are an ass, you fawning, time-serving Scalawag—what do you take me for?"

"For the criminal adventurer you are!" thundered the Judge.

"I'll not bandy words with you, Butler. I've

got you now, just where I want you. Five
minutes more of that Convention and you'll be a
memory as a politician. You never had a principle in your life. A professed leader of the
Republican party in the South composed of
Negroes, you loathe the very sight of a Negro.
You profess to be a Southerner, yet your ear is
always to the ground to hear the slightest whisper
from the lowest breed of Yankee demagogues
in the North. You lie to the Negro, you lie to
the Southern white man, you lie to the Yankee.
You're a pusillanimous, office-seeking turncoat
beneath the contempt of a man. Why did you
send for me?"

"To tell you that it's time for you to move on,
sir!" cried Butler with spluttering rage. "You
Carpetbag vultures have winged your way into
the South to tear from the loyal men of native
birth the rewards of their long patriotic services.
Go back to the slums and prison pens of the North
where you belong!"

"What do you mean?" Larkin broke in with
sudden energy.

"That you are a criminal adventurer, sir;
that's what I mean!"

Larkin laughed again.

"Is that all?"

"And I have in my pocket the documents to

prove that you have never acquired citizenship in the State of New York!"

"True, but irrelevant. I am a citizen now of this state under the Reconstruction Acts, and I'm going to represent the old commonwealth in the next Senate while you sink once more into the obscurity your feeble intelligence has prepared for you. Is this all you have to say?"

"No, sir, it's not!" whispered the Judge hoarsely with triumphant malice. "I have a letter in my pocket from the warden of the prison in England where you served your time, enclosing your photograph."

With a sudden cry of anguish Larkin leaped the distance separating them, gripped Butler by the throat, hurled him back in his seat, and held him strangling, spluttering, squirming in mortal terror. In a moment he released him, sank to a chair and buried his face in his hands.

"So! I am your master after all," the Judge sneered, recovering from his terror.

Larkin lifted his lion-like head a moment and looked at his opponent.

"Yes, I give up. I'll withdraw from the race if you'll keep my secret."

"I'll make no conditions with you sir; I mean to brand you a felon throughout the length and breadth of this land!"

"Not if you've an ounce of manhood in you,"
said the Carpetbagger with quiet dignity. "You
can't do it when I tell you the truth. Fifteen
years ago I was an honoured minister of the
gospel in Australia. An enemy of mine in England
published against me an infamous slander. I
returned to ask reparation. He not only refused
to give it but insulted me by a dastardly blow in
a public assembly. In a moment of insane rage
I returned his blow with one which resulted in his
death. Four months later I found myself, a man
of culture, refinement and the highest order of
social talents, a convict in prison garb serving a
sentence for manslaughter. I emerged more
dead than alive—it was late in life, but I lifted up
my head, sought a new world and began all over
again. Once more I've shown my power as a
leader of men. It was born in me—a God-given
birthright. My hair is white now with the frost of
the grave; I'm alone and friendless. Put yourself in my place. It's my last chance. You are
twenty years younger. I ask your pity, your
sympathy, your friendship.' Come, Judge, you
too are a soldier of fortune in conquered territory
and have your own secrets. Fight me fair."

"I'll fight you with every weapon in my power,
fair or foul. You're in my way; get out of it,"
sneered the Judge.

"You contemptible cur!" cried Larkin. "I could strangle you!"

"No doubt," sneered Butler. "If you dared!"

"Take care, you cowardly dog!" leaped the threat from the lips of the Carpetbagger, with a sudden flash of incontrollable rage; and again his massive figure towered over the Judge's slouching form. Butler's shifting eyes blinked in terror as he spluttered:

"I'll keep your secret on one condition!"

"What is it?" snapped Larkin.

"You're a man of genius. Use your talents for me, and we'll be friends."

"You have told no one the facts you have discovered?"

"No. Suggs knows only of the investigation as to your citizenship."

"I accept your terms," was the quiet answer.

The Convention ended in unexpected harmony, electing a solid Butler delegation. Larkin lingered in town for several days and, to the surprise and uneasiness of the Judge, stopped with Uncle Isaac in the little cottage by his gate.

CHAPTER VII

THE REIGN OF FOLLY

WITHIN two weeks Steve Hoyle's new Klan was organised and in absolute control of the Piedmont Congressional District.

John Graham saw that his defeat was a certainty and gave up the political fight in disgust. But he determined to prevent at all hazards the degradation of the Klan into an engine of personal vengeance and criminal folly. There was but one way to do it. He dreaded the undertaking, yet there was no help for it. He must again fight the devil with fire. The reign of terror inaugurated by the Black Union League had made necessary the Ku Klux Klan. There must be a power to hold in check Steve's irresponsible gang.

He immediately organised in each county a vigilance committee composed of the bravest and most reliable members of the old Klan who had refused to follow Steve. Over these men he sought to exercise only a moral influence as their former Commander-in-chief, save in his own county where his word was accepted as law by the surviving veterans of the regiment he had commanded in the Civil War.

These men he instructed to watch the movements of Steve's followers, learn in advance of their intended raids, break them up by moral suasion if possible; by force as a last resort.

He had found the task a tremendous one. For the first time he realised the terrible meaning of the lawless power of the Klan. The secrecy of their movements under his own leadership had been perfect. Yet with his knowledge of their methods he had believed it would be comparatively easy to defeat their plans. He found it next to impossible. In spite of the utmost vigilance on the part of his committees, the new Klan had inaugurated a reign of folly and terror unprecedented in the history of the whole Reconstruction saturnalia.

They whipped scalawag politicians night after night and drove them from the county. They called on carpetbagger postmasters who immediately left for parts unknown. They whipped Negroes, young and old, for all sorts of wrongdoing, real or fancied, and finally began to regulate the general morals of the community. They whipped a rowdy for abusing his wife and on the same night tarred and feathered a white girl of low origin who lived in the outskirts of town and ran her from the county.

The morning after this outrage occurred, John Graham walked into Steve's law office, brushed by his clerks and boldly entered the inner room where his enemy was at work.

Steve sprang to his feet and his hand instinctively sought the revolver in his hip pocket.

"You needn't be alarmed; I'm not ready for you yet," said John, his eyes holding Steve's with their steady light.

"Well, I'm ready for you," was the quick retort. "What do you want?"

"Merely to give you a little advice this morning."

"When I need your advice, I'll let you know."

John closed the door.

"Your men are covering the name of the Ku Klux Klan with infamy," John went on evenly. "If you have even the rudiments of common sense you must know that within a few weeks these fools will be beyond your control."

"I haven't felt the need of your help as yet," interrupted Steve.

"No, but I'm generous. I volunteer to anticipate the needs of your weak intelligence."

"John Graham," Steve broke in angrily, "if you have anything to say to me, say it, and get out of this room!"

"I will say it, my boy, and—don't—you—forget

it!" John answered with quiet emphasis, taking a step closer to his rival. "I'm close on the track of the men who are at present terrorising this county. I'll come up with them some night and there'll be business for the coroner next day. Dare to permit another outrage of a personal character in this county and I'll find your men if I drag the bottom of hell for them, and when I do, I'll hang them to a tree in front of your door. And—mark you—if I fail to find them I'll—hold—you—personally—responsible!"

Before Steve could reply he turned on his heel, slammed the door and left.

CHAPTER VIII

IMMEDIATELY following the interview with Steve the character of the raids of the new Klan changed to harmless pranks and practical jokes on impudent Negroes, scalawags and carpetbaggers, and John Graham observed it with a sigh of relief. Some of these escapades he could have enjoyed himself—particularly a call they made on the Apostle of Sanctification.

Uncle Isaac had greatly increased his prestige and following since the sensational speech he made in the County Convention and his public association with Larkin.

Following up his victory over the seven devils in Aunt Julie Ann, he had begun a series of revival meetings in the Northern Methodist church, calling its members to come up still higher. With each night his fervour and eloquence had increased. On this particular evening he attained unheard-of heights of inspiration, and announced not only his sinless perfection and his apostolic call, but the more startling fact that he was in daily personal communication with Jehovah himself. Amid a chorus of "Amens" and "Glory hallelujahs" from the sisters he boldly declared:

"Hear de Lawd's messenger! I come straight from him. De Lawd come every day ter my house. I sees him wid my own eyes. De debbil he doan pester me no mo. I'se de Lawd's sanctified one. I done wipe my weepin' eyes an' gone up on high. Will ye come wid me breddren an' sisters! I walk in de cool er de mawnin an' de shank er de even' wid de Lawd and de Lawd walks wid me. An' I ain't er skeered er nuttin in heaben above er hell below."

He had scarcely uttered the words when a white-robed ghost, fully ten feet high, walked solemnly down the aisle. There was a moment of awful silence. Isaac's jaw dropped in speechless terror. A sister in the amen corner screamed, and the Apostle sprang through the window behind the pulpit without a word, carrying the sash with him. In a minute the church was empty and the revival of Sanctification came to an untimely end.

It soon became the fashion for these merry masqueraders to call in groups on the pretty girls in town with the offer of their knightly protection. Frequently they spent the evening dancing and making merry, always in full disguise, guarding with the utmost care their identity. The mystery attending such visits, their secret signs and passwords, and the thrilling call of their whistles gave to these performances a peculiar atmosphere of romance and daring, and their visits came to be prized by the fair ones as tributes to their beauty and popularity.

A sign of invitation was devised by order of the leader of the raiders and posted one night on the bulletin board of the post office. The girl who wished the honour of such a call had only to express it by walking through the main street to the post office with a scarlet bow of ribbon tied on her left arm, and on the night following, promptly at ten o'clock, the knights on their white-robed horses would call.

Stella Butler had immediately become the most popular girl in Independence in spite of her father's politics. Her beauty was resistless. Every boy on whom she chose to smile was at once her friend and champion. The old Graham house became the most popular meeting place of the youth and beauty of the town, and the only men not welcome there were its real owner and his pugnacious younger brother.

Stella was fairly intoxicated with her social victory. Steve led in the devoted circle of her admirers, each day pressing his suit with humble and dogged persistence. She smiled in triumph at his abject surrender but continued to keep him at arm's length, showering her favours on all who were worth while.

She determined to crown her social leadership with a unique fancy dress ball by inviting the Klan masqueraders to dance with a select group of her girl friends at her home. The Klan itself was too deep a mystery for her to note the difference in the character of the raids since the night its gallant horsemen had cheered at her father's gate. She only knew in a general way that the Klan was born in the unconquered and unconquerable spirit of the old Bourbon South, the South of her mother, the only South worth cultivating socially.

So when the Judge's beautiful daughter, radiant and smiling, walked down the main street of Independence with the scarlet sign of the Klan on her left arm, she paralysed the business of the town. Every clerk stopped work and took his stand at the door or window until she was out of sight.

Her name was on every lip. If the raiders should accept her invitation, and appear at the old Graham mansion the evening following, the Judge would be in the anomalous position of a host who seeks the life of his guests. For the destruction of the Klan by exile, imprisonment and death had become the main plank in his political platform under Larkin's guidance.

Before Stella reached home the town was in a ferment of excitement to know whether the Judge had given his consent to this daring act. The older heads were sure that it was a child's thoughtless whim and that Butler would promptly and vigorously repudiate it.

John stood in the shadow by the window of his office and watched her pass in anguish. He saw in this invitation the complete triumph of the man he was coming to hate with deeper loathing than he had ever felt for her father. He was sure it was an inspiration of Steve Hoyle.

He observed old Larkin talking earnestly to Isaac on the other side of the street, and began to regret that the regiment of United States troops had been removed on the Carpetbagger's advice.

Were they here, he would suggest to the Judge that they be stationed about his home to-morrow night and those masked fools be kept out. He resented such a masquerade, not only because it was a travesty of the tragic drama in which he had played a part, but because he felt a deep sense of foreboding over the possible outcome of the affair. However harmless the intentions of the leaders of such a prank, there was always the chance of a drunken fool among them.

"My God," he exclaimed with a shiver of dread, "what will happen if the Judge in an ugly stupid temper encounters one of those masked fools maddened by drink!"

He sat down and hastily wrote a note of warning to Butler without a signature, tore it up in anger and threw it in his waste basket.

"Bah! it's nonsense!" he muttered in rage. "Her father is in no danger. The trouble is with me—I'm jealous, jealous, jealous! of the men who can see her. I want to dance with her myself. I'm mad with a passion I dare not breathe aloud."

Yet the longer he brooded over the thing, the keener became his sense of its dangers and the more oppressive the fear that it would result in a tragedy.

He sat down and rewrote his warning to the Judge, crossed the street and dropped the letter in the post office.

CHAPTER IX

A COUNTER STROKE

WHEN John returned to his desk he found Dan Wiley standing in the middle of the room pulling his long black moustache with unusual energy.

The young lawyer seated himself and motioned the mountaineer to a chair.

"No time ter fool."

"What's up?"

"Hell's afloat and the river's a risin!"

"Well?"

"Steve's gang from up in the hills in my township is on the way ter Independence. They're goin' ter raid old Sam Nickaroshinski, the Jew storekeeper, and rob 'im ter-night."

"Nonsense, Dan, they haven't got that low."

"Hit's jest like I tell ye. They're a gang of fightin' drunken devils. They'll do anything. I got a man to join 'em, an' he gimme the whole plot. Steve Hoyle don't know nothin' about it no more than their township leader does."

"Did you bring your men?" John asked.

"Yes, a half dozen. They ain't but six er

them skunks comin'. Our fellers are lyin' out
in the woods at the spring where we met you the
last time."

John leaped to his feet with a sudden resolution.

I'll join you at eight o'clock to-night and we'll
give the gentlemen from the hills an unexpected
reception." He seized his hat and closed his
office. As Dan turned to go he gave the low
quick order:

"Gags and ropes for six. Lay low and don't let
anybody know you're in town."

"I understand," said the mountaineer, with
a grin.

" John hurried home, and found to his annoyance
that Mrs. Wilson had gone buggy riding with
Billy and left the entire work of the house to
Susie.

"I hate to put more responsibility on your
beautiful young shoulders, Miss Susie," John
said hurriedly, "but I must beg you to stop your
work and make me a regalia for a little parade
to-night—you understand—will you do it?"

"With pleasure," was the smiling answer.
"I'll forgive Mama her idiotic trip with Billy
for this chance to serve you." She looked
tenderly into John's eyes.

Before sundown the costume was finished and
fitted to the tall figure by Susie's swift and gentle

hands and the last scrap of the cloth gathered up and piled in her work-basket before the first boarder arrived. Supper was an hour late, but Susie was singing at her work when Mrs. Wilson and Billy returned after dark.

Nickaroshinski's cottage was situated on the edge of a deep forest two miles out of town. It was a well-known fact that the old Jew walked to and from his store every morning and evening alone. And it was popularly believed that he hoarded his money under the floor of his bedroom.

Had any other man than Dan Wiley reported to John Graham such a projected raid, it would have been beyond his belief. The old Jew was on good terms with everybody. A refugee from Poland, his instinctive sympathies had always been with the oppressed people of the South, and to their cause he had faithfully given what influence he possessed.

The idea of such an atrocity by men wearing the uniform of his Klan roused John to the highest pitch of indignation. He was determined to make an example of these scoundrels that would not be forgotten.

The stars were shining brightly when he started with his men to the old Jew's place.

It was with a queer consciousness of the irony of fate that he galloped through the shadows to

strike horsemen who were wearing the uniform
of the mysterious order he had helped to create.
The wind freshened and grew chill, heavy clouds
obscuring the sky. The darkness became
intense.

He carefully placed his men in positions to
guard every approach to the house, and walked
to the door to warn the Jew of his danger and
arrange for the capture of the raiders.

A sudden crash and groan within told him only
too plainly that the scoundrels were already inside.

Gathering his men John closed in on the house.
As he expected they had put out no pickets, never
dreaming that they would be molested. They
had bound Nickaroshinski, beaten him unmercifully and tortured him until they had secured his
money and, not satisfied, had begun to smash things
to pieces.

Looking through the window John saw that
their costumes were exactly like his own and that
the six men had scattered through the house bent
on plundering every nook and corner. Knowing
that it would be impossible for them to distinguish
their own men from his, he made at once his plan
to capture the crowd without a struggle. Station-
ing his own six men at the front door, he took Dan
Wiley and boldly entered the room where the
leader stood covering the Jew with his revolver.

Without a word they walked toward him in the dim light.

Merely glancing at them the leader growled: "Finish up and let's get away from here!"

"All right," John answered coming closer, "I'm getting in a hurry myself."

Before he knew what they meant, Dan pounced on him and pinioned his arms while John quickly covered his mouth and fixed the gag.

It was but the work of a moment to tie the wretch and pass him out the door to the grim figures waiting. They repeated this performance in each room until all but two had been taken. These two were together. John suddenly blew his whistle giving the Klan signal "Follow me." When they entered the room two revolvers were suddenly thrust under their noses. They surrendered without a struggle.

John quickly released the old man, bound his wounds, restored his money and left with his prisoners.

Each of them were given forty lashes and the next morning when Steve Hoyle woke he found six stripe-marked half-naked men gagged and bleeding dangling by their arms from the limbs of the trees on his lawn. Around the neck of each hung a placard: "A warning to the scoundrels who are disgracing the uniform of the Ku Klux Klan in this county."

CHAPTER X

THE STRENGTH OF THE WEAK

STEVE HOYLE had cut down his men and hustled them out of town before eight o'clock, but the news rapidly spread and had thrown the people into a tremor of wonder as to the meaning of the events of the night. Evidently there had been a clash of forces within the ranks of the Invisible Empire. What did it mean?

Steve had lost no time in explaining to the desperadoes from the hills what they wished to know, and they had left with deep muttered curses against their former Commander-in-chief.

The outrage on Nickaroshinski had aroused the fiercest passions between the friends of John Graham and Steve Hoyle. Excited groups stood on every corner and it was with the utmost difficulty that John succeeded finally in dispersing them without a clash.

At one o'clock Larkin called at the old Graham mansion and announced to Aunt Julie Ann his desire to see the Judge.

"Ye can't see 'im," was her contemptuous answer.

Larkin had captured Isaac, but his influence had not reached his wife. For any white man who stayed at a Negro's house her contempt was beyond words. That the house happened to be her husband's only aggravated the offence.

"I must see him," urged Larkin.

"He's in bed sick, I tell ye!"

"But you had'nt told me," protested the Carpetbagger.

"Well I tells ye now. De Judge ain't lif' his head offen de piller ter-day. De ghosts wuz here agin las' night—an' you'd better be a movin' 'fore Miss Stella find you here. She sick de dog on you."

Larkin took a threatening step toward her and said in low tones:

"Shut your mouth, and tell the Judge I'm here to see him on important business. I'm not going out of this house until I do see him. Tell him so."

Aunt Julie Ann turned muttering and slowly climbed the stairs to Butler's room.

In a moment the Judge came down, hastily dressed in a faded slouchy dressing-gown and a pair of bedroom slippers.

"Is it possible," exclaimed Larkin," that you know nothing of what's happened here within the past twenty-four hours ?"

"I've been sick in bed. Haven't left the house," was the nervous reply.

"Well, it's time you knew at least what is going on in the house."

The Judge shivered and glanced up into the galleries.

"What do you mean?" he feebly asked.

Larkin rapidly sketched to him the events which had thrown the town into a ferment.

"But what I called for," observed the Carpetbagger, "was to enquire, as your political adviser, whether you really intend to permit your daughter to receive here to-night this gang of masked cutthroats as your guests?"

The Judge rose trembling.

"My daughter receive the Ku Klux Klan here to-night?" he gasped.

"She has invited them, and in spite of the excitement it is rumoured that they will promptly appear in full costume at ten o'clock."

"Impossible, Larkin, impossible! They won't dare such a thing. Besides, of course, my daughter will stop it."

"How can she stop it? Her invitation was by their sign of the scarlet bow. They have devised no signal to stop such a festival."

"She must find a way at once," cried the Judge excitedly, "otherwise we must wire for troops."

"It's too late."

"We'll order a special if necessary. I'll call my daughter at once."

Larkin rose as if to go.

"Wait," continued the Judge, "I wish you to be present."

He summoned Maggie, sent for Stella, and picked up his mail lying on the centre table, and opened it with fumbling nervous fingers while awaiting his daughter's appearance.

The Carpetbagger smiled contemptuously at his lack of good breeding, and studied the room while the Judge read his letters.

"I see here some friend has written me a warning against the dangers of such a meeting," cried Butler, his beady eyes dancing with excitement. "We must stop it, Larkin, we must stop it!"

Maggie slowly descended the stairs.

"Well, well, where's your mistress?" spluttered the Judge.

"Miss Stella say she busy tryin' on a dress an' she can't come now."

Butler turned on Maggie with sudden fury.

"Go back, you little black imp of the devil, and tell her to come down immediately! Immediately, I say!"

"Yassah! Yassah!" Maggie panted. She turned back up the stairs jumping three steps at

a time, and fell sprawling across the top landing.
She reached Stella's room gasping for breath.

Stella turned leisurely from her mirror.

"What on earth's the matter, Maggie?"

"De Jedge say ef you doan come dar dis minute
he gwine ter come up here and slap yo head off!"

"As bad as that, Maggie?"

"Yassam. He flung a big book at me an' hit
me right in the head jes case I tell 'im what you
say. Didn't ye hear it?"

Stella continued deliberately curling the ringlets
about the edges of her raven hair.

"Go back and tell him I'll be down in
a minute."

"Yassum. I spec he kill me dis time."

Stella finished her hair, sat down by the window
and read a novel for ten minutes and then slowly
descended the stairs.

The Judge sat slouching low in his chair, and
Larkin rose with the instinctive impulse of a
gentleman on Stella's appearance.

The girl stared coldly at her father, noted his
dressing-gown, turned hastily toward the stairs
and began to ascend.

"Excuse me," she said to him with pointed
insolence, "I thought you were waiting to
receive me."

"Look here, my child, I've no time for silly

nonsense!" the Judge exclaimed, adjusting the folds of his slouchy robe.

"When you have completed your toilet," she said with a sneering little smile, "I'll come at once. Please let me know."

"Stella!" sternly called her father.

The girl continued without turning her head and disappeared on the floor above.

"A stickler for social forms, Larkin," said the Judge petulantly, rising.

"I see," said the Carpetbagger with amusement.

"I'll have to humour her. Wait for me. We must stop it."

When at length the Judge returned and confronted Stella he was unnerved, while she stood staring at him with a hard glitter in her great brown eyes, complete mistress of every faculty she possessed.

"My child," began Butler, "Larkin tells me that you have invited the Ku Klux raiders to dance here to-night."

"I have," was the cool answer.

"But my dear, you should have consulted me."

"You made me the mistress of this house; why should I consult you about a harmless social gathering of my friends?"

"The Klan is a secret order of assassins and desperadoes."

"Please father, don't!" she interrupted. "Your politics disgust me. These boys are of the best families in town."

"How can you know this?" pleaded the Judge.

"They come disguised. Not one of them has ever made himself known."

"Which makes the romance of such a visit all the deeper."

"And its dangers all the greater, my child. Mr. Larkin has come to warn me."

"I agree with your father, Miss Stella," said Larkin with a grave bow.

The girl tossed her head with contempt.

"And I have in my hand a letter of warning from an unknown friend," continued Butler.

"But you are not really afraid?" cried the girl with scorn. "I refuse to believe my own father the contemptible coward your enemies have called you."

"Have you heard of the criminal outrages committed last night by those masked raiders?"

"They do not interest me."

"You must remember, my dear, that I have sworn to send these men to the gallows."

"I can't help your political bluster. I refuse to sacrifice my social career and insult my friends for your dirty politics."

"And you can not see that the presence of

these masked men in this house would be a mortal insult to me?"

"Certainly not. A crowd of gay masqueraders who come to do me honour."

"You must stop it, my child."

"It is impossible now. My friends are getting ready. I've hired a band."

"You refuse to respect my wishes?"

"I refuse to make a fool of myself!"

"Come, my dear, you must be reasonable. I know I've spoiled you. I've loved you too well. I've indulged every whim of your heart and allowed you to rule me, but you can't do this absurd and dangerous thing. You forget that you are not only making a fool of me but that you are putting my life in jeopardy."

"I'll assume the responsibility!" she broke in, drawing herself up with pride. "If you receive the slightest insult or a hair of your head is harmed I'll give my life to avenge it."

"You persist?" asked her father with a scowl.

"I do," flashed the answer.

The Judge rose, hesitated a moment and then said with stern determination:

"Then for the first time in my life, I forbid you a thing on which you have set your heart. These masked men shall not enter my house!"

Stella's eyes flashed fire.

"They shall come!" she cried.

"Larkin," said the Judge, turning to the Carpetbagger, "I shall have to ask you to go to the telegraph office and order the troops here on a special. Ask them to protect me to-night from these assassins."

Stella's figure suddenly stiffened with incontrollable rage. She clenched her fists and sprang in front of her father screaming.

"Don't you dare insult me by applying such epithets to my friends! If you are my father, you are a poltroon and a coward!"

"Stella, my darling!" gasped the Judge.

"Don't you call me darling! Don't you dare to speak to me again! I'll leave this house and blot your very name from my memory!"

Butler staggered back in dumb amazement and Larkin watched with a curious smile playing about the corners of his piercing eyes.

Stella stamped her foot, turned, and bounded up the stairs and into her room, slammed the door and began to scream.

The Judge stood for a moment in speechless horror. He had never crossed her imperious will before and he was utterly unprepared for her mad outburst. He loved her with all the tenderness of which his low nature was capable, and had never seen a woman in hysterics. He had therefore no standard by which to measure how much of pure devil and how much of real suffering were mingled in her cries. Each piercing scream tore his heart. He turned helplessly to Larkin and asked:

"What shall I do?"

"Excuse me Judge, I can't advise you in such a matter," the Carpetbagger replied. "But I think you'll have to summon a doctor."

"My God, is she in danger?" he asked, in a stupor of pain. "I'll go up and see."

He shuffled up the stairs as quickly as possible, and hurried into her room without knocking.

Stella sprang from the bed where she lay moaning, laughing and crying, and flew at him, stamping and screaming:

"Don't you come near me. Don't you touch me! Don't you speak to me! Get out of this room!"

"But my dear," stammered the Judge.

"Get out of this room—get out of this room! or I'll jump out of that window and kill myself!"

She seized him by the arm, hustled and pushed him out of the door, slammed and locked it. Again she threw herself on the bed and burst into strangling groans.

The Judge retreated to the hall below, his eyes filled with tears, his heart sick with terror. He dropped into a seat, covered his face with his hands and sat for a moment in stupid pain.

Maggie suddenly plunged down the stairs yelling:

"Goddermighty, ye better run fur de doctor quick—Miss Stella dying! She done choke ter death!"

"I'll bring the doctor," said Larkin, rising quickly.

"Run and bring Aunt Julie Ann!" whispered the Judge to Maggie.

The maid met Aunt Julie Ann who had heard the commotion and the two hurried back to Stella's room.

When the doctor came she refused to see him, and he left in a rage. The Judge begged Larkin to stay until he could see his daughter.

An hour later, propped up in bed with Maggie rubbing one hand and Aunt Julie Ann the other, she permitted her father to enter and receive her pardon. The Judge knelt by the bedside, kissed her hand and wet it with tears. His surrender was abject. He sent Larkin away and promised to be present at the ball and treat the whole thing as a schoolboys' frolic.

And then she smiled and kissed him.

"If I'm only strong enough to dress by ten o'clock!" she cried, laughing.

"Try to eat something, dear," urged her father.

She promised and asked Aunt Julie Ann to

send her a little soup. She got the soup and with it a substantial meal.

Still and catlike, Maggie watched her eat it down to the last crumb with quiet enjoyment. When the black maid picked up the tray she walled her eyes first at the empty dishes and then at her wonderful little mistress and softly giggled.

CHAPTER XI

A S THE hour approached for the masqueraders to appear at the Judge's John Graham
was drawn to the spot by an irresistible impulse.
He stood in the shadows of the trees on the sidewalk and watched the little squadron of white
and scarlet horsemen wheel into the gate past
Isaac's cottage, and gallop swiftly up to the front
door of the old mansion.

They had scarcely passed when Isaac suddenly
stepped from the shrubbery through the open
gateway and ran into him.

The Apostle gasped in terror:

"De Lawd, marse John, I thought you wuz one
er dem ghostes—'scuse me, sah, I'se er gettin'
away from here!"

John made no reply, merely watching him until
he disappeared.

Again he turned toward the house. Every
window was gleaming with light. The subdued
strains of a string band came stealing through the
trailing roses on the porch, and he fancied he
could catch the odour of the flowers in their sweet

notes. Scarcely knowing what he did, he strolled into the lawn and sank on a rustic bench with a groan. He could hear the gay banter of the masqueraders and the peals of girlish laughter with which their tomfoolery was being received.

A mocking bird began singing in the tree above him, roused by the music of the band. Far off in the corner of the lawn in the clump of holly and cedars at the entrance of the vault a whippoorwill was making the ravine ring with the weird notes of his ghost-like call. The moon flooded the scene with silvery splendour. Crushed with a sense of loneliness and failure, he felt to-night that he would give all the wealth and honours of the earth for one touch of the hand of the girl whose laughter lingered and echoed in his heart. And again the feeling of impending disaster overwhelmed him.

"Of course it's nonsense!" he kept repeating to himself. "The disaster is within. I'm merely a wounded animal caught in a trap, bleeding and dying of thirst, and no one knows or cares, and I can't cry for help."

He tried to rise and go. But something held him in a silent spell to the spot. He sat dreaming out each movement of the gay drama in progress within.

Stella had welcomed her white-robed guests without the aid of a servant. No Negro could be hired for love or money to approach one of these ghostly figures. Maggie had hidden in the closet in her mistress' room and Aunt Julie Ann had barred herself inside the kitchen and refused to answer a call.

In spite of these little annoyances the beautiful young mistress of the Graham house, resplendent in her ball dress costume, was in her gayest mood.

When the shrill whistles rang their summons at the door, she hastened to greet her mysterious guests.

"And your name, Sir Knight?" she asked the leader with bantering laughter.

"We are Ghouls! And come from beyond the river Styx, my lady!" solemnly answered the tall white figure.

"Welcome shades of Darkness, welcome back to the world of joy and light, song and dance, life and love!" Stella cried, extending her hand.

When they had tied their horses to the posts beside the wide driveway they slowly entered single file into the great hall. Stella, assisted by Susie Wilson, who had become her fast friend, greeted each of them with words of gay welcome.

They were dressed in the regulation raider's costume of the Klan. The white flowing ulster-like robe came within three inches of the floor. A scarlet belt circled the waist, from either side of which hung heavy revolvers in leather holsters. A dagger was attached to the centre of the belt, and the scarlet-lined white cape thrown back on the shoulders revealed their militant trappings with startling distinctness. On each breast was wrought the emblem of the Invisible Empire, the scarlet circle, and in its centre a white cross. Spiked helmets of white cloth with flowing masks reached to the cape on each shoulder, completely covering the head and face. With red gauntlets to complete their costume, the disguise was absolute. The only visible part of the body was the eye, gleaming with a strange steady supernatural brilliance through the holes cut in the mask. It was a curious fact that all eyes looked alike in the shadows of these trappings at night. They were simply flashing points of living light with all traces of colour lost in the shadows.

In spite of the fact that the girls felt they had nothing to fear from the white figures, it was with a tremor of excitement they each greeted the mysterious partners of their dance.

Stella left them talking romantic nonsense of knights and tournaments, ghouls and ghosts in the hall and ran up to her father's room.

"Oh! Papa," she cried with childish glee. "It's such fun! They're all here. You will come down and join the party as you promised?"

"Yes, yes, dear, I'll come, presently," said the Judge with evident dread.

Stella slipped her beautiful bare arm around his neck and her cheek rested against his, while the soft little fingers found his hand.

"I'm awfully sorry I was so ugly to-day," she said gently. "But I couldn't help it. I didn't know I had such a temper. I must have gotten it from you Dad."

"It's all right, my darling, if you'll never say such bitter things to me again—will you?" he asked tenderly, tears filling his eyes.

"No, I'll be good now, if you'll forgive me?"

Her father answered with a kiss. "You see, you're all I have in the world, my little girlie. I'm not as strong as I used to be. I don't think I'm going to live long."

"Rubbish! you've just got the blues. Shake them off and be young again to-night. Imagine you are a boy here with mother the sweetheart you're trying to steal from the proud rich people who hate you—come, come!"

The Judge smiled in spite of himself. Her mood was contagious. He stroked her hand gently.

"I'll be down right away. Run on and have a good time."

"All right, I'll start the first dance and you'll be

there by the time it's over and shake hands with your enemies. It will be so jolly!"

Throwing him a kiss she returned to the hall below and led her guests into the big double parlours which had been fitted up for dancing. The French windows, opening as doors on the porches, were raised, and the band stationed outside near one of them.

When the dance had begun the Judge, dressed in his usual broadcloth frock coat which hung in slouching lines from his drooping shoulders, slowly descended the stairs and stood embarrassed and hesitating in the hall a moment, and sat down by the centre table.

A masquerader came in from the ball room for the fan his partner had left, and so soft was his footfall the Judge did not hear or see him until the tall white figure suddenly loomed above him to pick up the fan.

The apparition was so startling the Judge's nerves collapsed. He leaped to his feet with an inarticulate cry of terror, overturning his chair and started to bolt for the door.

The masquerader smothered a laugh and said:

"I beg your pardon, I only wanted the fan."

Butler stammered:

"Ah—I—must have been dreaming—you—startled me!"

He watched the white figure disappear, mopped the perspiration from his brow, called Aunt Julie Ann and ordered her to bring him a drink of whiskey. She refused to stir at first, but he threatened to discharge her, and she obeyed.

When the Judge raised the glass to his lips his hand trembled so violently that he spilled some of the liquor on his clothes. He gulped it down and glanced nervously about the hall.

He placed the glass back on the tray and Aunt Julie Ann, watching the parlour-door like a hawk, started back to the kitchen on a run.

"Wait a moment," cried the Judge, shuffling to his feet.

"I ain't gwine stay in here wid dem things in de house," she answered, halting timidly in the shadows of the door leading into the dining-room.

Butler walked to her side and said:

"Tell Miss Stella I'm not feeling well—I'm going to bed."

He hesitated a moment. "You've said nothing to any one about this ghost business?"

"Hush, man, hush! Don't talk about dat now!" she whispered. "I tole dat ole white-headed Larkin—dat's all."

"Well, I want to warn you, don't mention it to another living soul. I'm beginning to suspect that we've been seeing old Major Graham himself!"

"De Lawd er mussy, man, how he bin gittin' in de house wid all de doors and windows locked an' bolted?"

"That's a mystery I can't fathom."

"No, ner nobody else. Hit's his sperit I tells ye."

While they were talking thus in the alcove the oak panel under the stairs was softly opened and closed; old Major Graham, dressed with scrupulous care, thin and pale as a corpse, yet erect and dignified, walked slowly across the hall to the foot of the stairs. His lips were muttering inarticulate sounds and his wide staring eyes had the far-off look of the dreamer who lives, breathes and moves, yet sees nothing.

Butler's back was to the Major, and Aunt Julie Ann, hearing the footsteps, was first to see him. She staggered against the wall and gasped:

"God, save us, dar he is now!"

Butler glanced over his shoulder and backed against the huge figure of the cook, trembling.

"Look—look!" he whispered. "It *is* old Graham. Watch his thin bony fingers grip the rail as he climbs the steps!"

"Hit's his livin' ghost I tell ye!" persisted Aunt Julie Ann. "He'll walk right out on de roof an' step off'n de house des like he does every night—you won't see' 'im again."

"Get some more whiskey!" said the Judge. "I'll go with you"—he added, following her into the dining room, mopping the perspiration from his brow.

"I'll go up there in a minute and find out the truth!"

"Better keep outen dat attic I tells ye. Dey say dat de ghosts er de livin' is wuss dan de dead."

They had scarcely passed from the hall when the oak panel again opened and a white masked figure peered through, and quickly entered.

The dress was an exact duplicate of the masqueraders down to its minutest details, and only the closest observer would have noted the awkward way in which the figure moved as though not in the habit of walking in his disguise.

He quickly glanced about the hall, listened a moment to the sounds of revelry in the ballroom, closed the door of the small hall leading into it, reopened the panel and signalled.

In rapid succession eight more silent figures filed through the panel door. The leader whispered to his followers:

"He's in the dining room. Guard every entrance now but that."

In a moment a masked man stood guard at each door and the leader lowered the lamp on the table until only the dim outlines of the forms could be seen, and stepped back himself into the shadows of the alcove by the dining room door.

Aunt Julie Ann returned to the kitchen, and the Judge, afraid to go upstairs, came back into the hall to enter the ballroom as he promised Stella.

As he passed through the door of the dining room the shrouded figure standing in the alcove quickly followed, cutting off this retreat.

The Judge stopped, blinked his eyes around the dim hall and muttered:

"Why, why, the lamp's gone out!" He quickly crossed the space to the table and extended his hand to turn up the lamp.

The figure behind him seized his arm and a guttural voice spoke through the mask:

"There's light enough for our work, Judge."

Butler staggered back in terror and glanced about him at the dim spectres closing around the table. With an effort he pulled himself together and stammered:

"Why, of course, boys. I see! I see! You're going to initiate me! give me the third degree first —I see—a good joke!"

"You'll find it a serious joke before you're through," replied the leader, gripping his dagger.

The Judge could see the movement of his hand as he slowly drew the knife from its sheath, the blade glistening for an instant in the dim lamplight, but he still thought the boys were playing a prank on him.

"Well, gentlemen, have your fun!" he cried with forced gaiety, "Have your way, I'm at your service. What is the penalty I must pay to-night for my many sins against the Klan?"

"The penalty is your life," said the mask with sullen menace in his tones, stepping closer, "unless you agree to leave this state to-morrow and never enter it again—will you go?"

"So bad as that?" The Judge forced a laugh. "What else?"

"You are not fooling with boys now!" sullenly said the towering white form. "Give me your answer, you d——d old sneaking coward! Will you go or do you prefer to die?"

Butler, trembling now with mingled terror and rage, cried angrily:

"Gentlemen, your joke is going too far!"

"It'll go farther," was the quick reply, as the white figures closed in threateningly and the foremost man moved as if to raise his hand.

"Enough of this! Get out of my house!" Butler suddenly shouted, snatching the mask from the leader's head by a quick unexpected display of courage. A cry of horror and surprise leaped from his lips. The knife flashed, and was buried in his heart. He reeled, staggered, clutched a chair and sank with a groan to a sitting posture. His long awkward arms drooped and his head sank slowly on his breast.

The leader, who had quickly replaced his helmet, bent over him a moment, sheathed his knife and said:

"A good stroke—all right—quick now—open the doors and follow me."

The guard at the door leading into the ballroom opened it gently and the sweet strains of the music rang through the hall with startling distinctness, as the white-masked figures slowly disappeared through the panel under the stairs.

Aunt Julie Ann who had heard the Judge's cry and the sudden noise entered trembling.

"Name er God what's dis!" she cried. "De light gone out! De ghost done dat!"

She turned up the lamp and saw the Judge sitting dead in the chair, the scarlet stain on his clean ruffled shirt holding her for a moment in speechless horror.

Screaming at last, she rushed to the ballroom door and shouted:

"De Lawd hab mussy! De ghost done kill de Judge—Stab 'im fro de heart!"

The music stopped with a crash and the crowd rushed into the hall.

Stella stared at the lifeless form, her beautiful

face whiter than the dead, turnec. to the masqueraders huddled in a group, drew herself proudly erect, pointed to the door and said:

"Go!"

Silently and quickly they left, and as the last beat of their horses' hoofs died away in the distance she lifted her face from her father's hand which she had covered with kisses, and groaned:

"Forgive me—forgive me!   I have but one aim in life now—God give me strength!"

"Stella stared at the lifeless form"

Book II—A Woman's Revenge

CHAPTER I

STELLA'S RESOLUTION

THE murder of Judge Butler created a profound sensation both in the state and the nation. The Northern press held the Ku Klux Klan guilty of this atrocious crime without question, and it was the last straw needed to start an avalanche of hostile legislation in Congress against the entire South.

The famous Conspiracy Act was rushed through both houses of the National Legislature and signed by the President. It made membership in the secret order known as the Ku Klux Klan, or Invisible Empire, a felony, and provided for the trial of its members on the charge of treason, conspiracy and murder. The President was authorised to suspend the writ of *habeas corpus* and proclaim martial law in any county of the Southern States, and use the army and navy to enforce his authority.

The Attorney General promptly placed the county of Independence under military government, stationed two regiments of troops within its borders, and set to work with scores of detectives to find the guilty man.

Two months passed without the slightest progress. Five thousand dollars reward was offered by the national authorities and a similar sum by the state. Not a trace of the man responsible for the deed could be found, though a price of ten thousand dollars was set thus on his head. A number of arrests had been made, but the evidence produced was of so flimsy a character that in each instance the prisoner could not be held.

The longer the case was probed, the deeper became its insoluble aspects. The "Butler Murder Mystery," as it was popularly known, provoked the widest public discussion, both in the state and national press, yet no explanation from any quarter could be found.

The effects of the crime on the Ku Klux raiders was immediate. Not a trace of their existence was left. The enormity of the tragedy had evidently sobered the dare-devils who had found amusement or personal profit in its activities. It now became the fashion to denounce the Klan and demand its extermination.

As the order had never had a spokesman, it had no defender. The demand for its suppression was universal. Yet no traitor had appeared among its ranks. The deepest curses of a race were reserved for the white lip that should betray its members. Whatever the leaders of public opinion might say, the masses of the people knew the necessity which had called this dreaded order into existence—the black threat of Negro dominion. Thousands of women and children knew its secrets and held them inviolate.

On Stella Butler the death of her father had wrought a deep and remarkable change. The fun-loving, imperious, self-willed, spoiled child had suddenly become a serious woman. She had given every hour of her time assisting the authorities in their search for the murderer and had followed every possible clue with breathless hope.

Two forces had driven her into a morbid interest in the crime, pride and remorse. In mere laughing banter she had promised her father if a single insult should be offered him, or a hair of his head harmed, she would give her life to avenge the deed. She had not dreamed of such a possibility. But now that the impossible had happened, she would make good her word to the dead. And she would make it good, not only because she had promised and her heart was sick with remorse for the part she had unconsciously played in the tragedy, but for a deeper personal reason—the consciousness of the insult to her pride which the crime had offered. The assassin had dared to strike her father dead in her home, in her very presence.

Had the knife sought her own heart she would have felt less deeply the wound. Somewhere even by her side there stood amid the shadows of life a being who could thus insult her by ignoring her very existence! She resolved to make that man feel her power by paying the penalty with his own life. An element of pitiless cruelty in her character found for the first time its expression in a passionate thirst for the blood of this criminal.

She had seen every effort to penetrate the mystery fail with increasing inward rage. Larkin, who had charge of the Judge's campaign, had been aggressive and untiring for two weeks and then had given up and returned to his duties as Chairman of the State Executive Committee.

The Attorney General announced his departure for Washington and ordered the withdrawal of the troops and detectives.

Stella hastened to send her burning protest against his action. General Champion, who had been deeply moved by her beauty and evident suffering, called personally at the old Graham mansion for an interview. He received her indignant protests with the gravest courtesy.

"Please don't tell me, General," she began bitterly, "that my father's death is an apparently insoluble mystery.   I am sick, sick, sick of hearing such rubbish! Eight weeks ago he was murdered in cold blood in this hall on the very spot where you are now sitting.   It was not done by ghosts, it was not an accident, it was done by a living man. I refuse to recognise in it an act of Providence. I will not wear an emblem of mourning as long as this man breathes on earth.   I have sworn it My father was in the service of his country attempting to enforce its laws.   I have the right to demand that a rich and powerful government avenge his death.   It is incredible that the coward who did this crime can not be caught and punished."

"Upon the other hand, my dear child," said the General, "I assure you that the apprehension of this criminal is one of the most difficult tasks ever assigned the Department of Justice."

"And why, pray?"

"Because in this climate the Invisible Empire is yet stronger than the visible——"

"You believe then that the Klan committed the deed?" she asked

"As sure of it as that I live.   If we were dealing with the ordinary criminal, it would be easy.   We are dealing with larger problems.   Every clue we have found has proven false for this reason. The man really responsible stands at our elbow did we but know the truth."

"What do you mean?" Stella asked with sudden interest.

"That your father's death was ordered by an inner circle of the Invisible Empire. He was probably executed by an individual who did not even know his name. The occasion of the masquerade ball was simply utilised for the purpose. Unless we know the name of the Chief of the Klan in this state no progress can be made. This man has the power of life and death over his men. No such deed could have been committed without his order."

"And you are going to give up the search?" was the eager question.

"For the present yes. It is a waste of time."

"And you have formed no idea as to who this Chief may be?" asked the big brown eyes, flashing with a new purpose.

"I haven't a scrap of evidence that can be used in an English-speaking court of justice—but I am morally certain that I know the man."

"And if you knew him by his own confession?"

"I could send him to the gallows within thirty days."

"The man you suspect?"

"John Graham!"

Stella sprang to her feet, her face white with an

emotion which stopped for a moment her very heart-beat.

"Within a month I'll tell you the truth"—she said with laboured breath.

"Can you do it?"

"Beyond the shadow of a doubt!" was her firm answer.

The General seized her hand as he took his leave.

"If you do, my child, you will destroy an empire mightier than the law of the land. I'll place the entire resources of the Department of Justice at your command."

Stella's brown eyes rested on her own beautiful reflection in the mirror as she slowly said:

"Thank you, General, I have at present all the weapons I shall need."

CHAPTER II

WEIGHED AND FOUND WANTING

STELLA was putting the last touches to a perfect toilet before meeting Steve Hoyle who was waiting impatiently below. She had given him the sign for which he had long prayed, her permission for the formal renewal of his suit. They had remained friends on condition that he keep silent on the subject until she gave him permission to speak. She had done this in the most delicate way in the note of reply she had sent in the afternoon to his request for permission to call.

She had determined to take Steve by storm to-night. The secret on which her heart was set she counted already within her grasp, yet she would leave no stone unturned, neglect no trick in all the known realm of woman's art to make her victory absolute.

Her refusal to put on black at her father's funeral, or wear it since, and her declaration that his death was not the act of God but of the devil, had shocked the tradition-loving Southern people beyond measure. Maggie had lost no time in telling her their comments. She heard them with contempt and proceeded to shock her critics still worse by establishing herself permanently in the great lonely house with only Aunt Julie Ann as her guardian.

Her whole being was fused into a single deathless purpose—to take the life of the man who had killed her father. She would stop at no means to accomplish this end, and she would treat with scorn every convention of society which might interfere.

She slowly descended the winding stairs to-night before Steve's enraptured gaze, dressed in pure white with full train. A single deep red rose was set in her black hair. Her arms were bare and their beauty was perfect—starting with the tiniest wrists and swelling into full voluptuous splendour above the dimpled elbows. She had a way of moving them when she walked which was modest yet subtle in sensuous suggestion.

Steve watched her spellbound. She placed her hand in his with a tender smile, the brown eyes watching the effects of her beauty with quiet triumph.

She allowed Steve to silently lead her to the old davenport under the stairs and take his seat by her side.

"You meant what your letter implied?" he asked eagerly.

"I did," was the firm answer.

"It seemed too good to be true, dear, yet I felt sure that you would need me in this crisis of your life."

"I do need you. I wonder if you will prove wanting when put to the test?"

"Try me!" he boldly challenged.

"You are sure that you love me with a love that will endure through good and evil, through life and death, through every test?"

She leaned close, her eyes searching Steve's soul.

The man drew a deep breath and his hand grasped hers with fierce passion.

"I love you beyond the power of words to tell—I worship you!" he cried, attempting instinctively to draw her into his arms.

"Yes I know," she answered, lifting her hand in warning, "you love me that way—I don't say it displeases me—I have a soul and I have a body too. There's something big, fierce, and strong in you, Steve, that always drew me—that draws me to you to-night—but I want to know if your love goes deeper than the body; if it's big enough, true enough to dare anything in this world or the next for the woman you love?"

"Yes!" he cried.

"You love me better than money?"

"Yes!"

"Better than power?"

"Yes!"

"Better than your own life?"

"Yes!" he whispered, crushing her hand in his.

"Suppose I should put you to a test and you should fail?"

"With your eyes calling me I'd dare the terrors of hell!"

She took both his hands, fixed her eyes on his until their warm brown light enfolded him with tenderness:

"Give me the name of the Chief of the Ku Klux Klan in North Carolina," she whispered.

Steve's face went white, and he stammered:

"Why—why—my dear—how—can—I? I don't know him. It's impossible!"

"Nothing is impossible to the man who loves me if I desire it," she answered, firmly holding Steve with her eyes dilated to extraordinary size under the tension of her deep emotion.

He turned from her gaze, the cold sweat breaking out on his forehead.

"But, Stella, my dear, I'm not a member of the Klan."

She dropped his hand, sprang to her feet, and looked at him a moment.

"You are lying!"

"I swear I'm telling you the truth," he cried, eagerly attempting to regain her hand.

She turned from him with contempt. She saw too late that she had overplayed the part. She had been too eager, too sure. He was a greater coward than she had suspected.

"But why should you ask such a thing of me?" he stammered.

"You know why."

"I haven't the remotest idea."

"Coward!" she hissed, turning suddenly. "You know that I wish to hang this man for the murder of my father."

"If the Government of the United States with its army and navy and its millions cannot find him —am I a coward because I tell you that I do not know his name?"

"Yes."

"In God's name why?" he pleaded.

"I know that you are a member of the Klan."

"Upon my soul and honour I swear that I am not!"

"Have you either soul or honour?"

"I won't quarrel with you, dear; you are over-wrought and crushed by this tragedy. You don't mean what you say."

"I do mean it!" she fiercely cried.

"Then you'll live to regret it," he answered, recovering his composure. "I'll do anything within human reason. You must not ask the impossible."

"Then you will help me to find this man?"

"To the limit of my power."

"Why say to the limit of my power? I hate a man who fences, squirms and lies when face to face with a test of his manhood! Will you help me find this man? Yes or no?"

"Yes."

"That's better."

"But tell me," he said, watching her with increasing reserve and cunning. "Whom do you suspect?"

"John Graham."

Steve's eyes flashed.

"And what is your programme when you have established the fact?"

"The Attorney General has promised to hang him within thirty days."

"With all due respect to the Attorney General —he can't do it."

"Why not?"

"We are living under conditions of revolution. No jury can be found who will convict him. There's but one way."

"What do you mean?" Stella asked, lowering her voice.

"That beyond a doubt John Graham inspired this crime."

"You believe it?" she broke in fiercely.

"I'm sure of it. His hatred of the Judge had become a mania. He used the Klan as the cloak of his hired assassin."

"The Klan decreed his death," said Stella sternly.

"John Graham decreed it."

"What do you propose?" she asked, again coming close to Steve.

"To have him executed by the Klan itself!"

"And yet you are not a member?" she asked with a smile.

"I am in touch with men who are."

"How could his execution be brought about?"

"Ask him the question you put to me."

"And if he tells?"

"He will forfeit his life."

Stella's eyes rested a moment on the chair in which her father fell the night of his death. She turned and gazed into Steve's face with a strange absent expression in her eyes as though they were seeing a picture which had etched itself in fire on her soul.

"I'm going to cultivate Mr. Graham's

acquaintance," she slowly said. "I'll learn from his own lips if he is the leader of the Ku Klux Klan."

"And if you find that he is?"

"I may hold you to your pledge!"

"And on the day he is executed."

"I will marry you!"

CHAPTER III

THE next morning Steve Hoyle left town and
Stella began at once to put into execution
her plan to entrap John Graham in the meshes
of her beauty and deliver him to justice. She
felt instinctively that if this man with his intense
and romantic nature ever yielded to the spell of her
love, there could be no limit to which he would
not go at her bidding. With equal certainty she
realised that the task would be a delicate one—a
task which might put to the test every power she
possessed. Her whole being rose to the work
with a thrill of keen, cruel interest—the interest
of the primitive huntress on track of the rarest,
wildest and most daring game.

The first difficulty which apparently opened an
impassable gulf between them was the suit which
John Graham had begun to regain possession of
the estate. The language in which his complaint
had been drawn was the limit of bitter accusation
permitted in a legal document—parts of it, indeed,
the Court had ordered stricken from the record
as scandalous and irrelevant.

Stella's eyes danced with excitement as she read in the morning's paper the announcement of his withdrawal of this suit. The news was accompanied by a brief statement which might have been written as a personal apology to her for the language he had used.

"I beg leave to say to the public in withdrawing this action that I regret the overheated language in which the original complaint was expressed."

Without a moment's hesitation she seized her pen and wrote him an invitation to call. Her words revealed the deeply laid scheme on which her mind had seized in a flash of inspiration. She read and reread it carefully:

My dear Mr. Graham:

Permit me to thank you for the manly words of retraction which you have used in this morning's paper. Your withdrawal of this suit and the generous manner in which it was done, removes the only barrier to our friendly acquaintance. I wish to renew it, and ask you to please accept at once the position of my personal attorney in the settlement of my father's estate. Your influence in the courts of North Carolina, your eloquence and genius will be of invaluable service to an orphan girl who needs the advice of one on whose integrity she can absolutely rely.

Trusting that you may honour me by answering this request in person at three o'clock this afternoon,

Sincerely,

Stella Butler.

John Graham could not believe his senses when he first read this letter. The boy had turned and gone without waiting for an answer and he sat stupefied by a whirl of conflicting emotions.

He read it again, bent and kissed her name. He had never before seen her handwriting. He studied it with curious interest. Its deep lines revealed with startling distinctness traits of a remarkable character. It was full of long strokes of the pen with equal emphasis across, up and down. The letters were unevenly formed, showing the self-willed, imperious spirit that had refused to copy the lines set by another hand, and yet the effect was pleasing and held the eye in a continuous surprise at its sensational curves and dashes. Through every line he felt the throb of an intense nature, which seemed to sink into inaudible whispers of emotion in the queer little twists of the pen with which each sentence ended.

He placed the note in an inner pocket. Had he received this invitation yesterday, he would have locked his doors, shouted and danced for joy at the opportunity to press her hand again and look into those deep brown eyes that haunted him waking or dreaming. Now it was a serious question. Within twenty-four hours he had received confirmation of two suspicions which had oppressed him since the night of Butler's death—

that his father might have committed the deed and that Billy was in the party of masqueraders.

In either case, the stain of the Judge's blood was on the house of Graham and the Angel of Death stood with drawn sword barring the way of his happiness. He would not seek the hand of Stella with the blood of her father on his own. He would accept the moral responsibility of his father's act or that of his younger brother. He had reproached himself bitterly that he had neglected to know and teach his high-strung younger brother as he might. The mother dead, his father a hopeless mental invalid, Billy had grown up with no hand to guide his wayward fancy. It was not to be wondered at that he soon recognised no authority save that of his own will.

Stella's request had brought John face to face with the problems of his father and Billy. He must know the truth before he could answer that letter. Better to strangle the love that was fast swelling in his heart than wait until the hour when the call of love might drown the voice of honour.

He left his office and went at once to his father's room. The Major was dressed with his habitual care, his linen spotless, his boots carefully polished, his thin white hair brushed straight back from his high forehead. He was seated in his armchair, gently stroking with his chalk-white bony hand

his delicate ghostly beard, while delivering to
Alfred one of his interminable talks of the old life
in the South. At times he forgot the war and the
horrors which followed and reenacted the scenes
of the past until his former slave, too full to bear
more, would stop him tenderly, and get him to
change the subject.

"Leave us awhile, Alfred," John said, on
entering.

"Yassah," the old butler answered, bowing
himself out with stately dignity.

John closed the door and drew his chair close
to the Major's.

"Father, I want to ask you something very
particular," be began.

The old man smiled indulgently.

"Well, out with it, you young rascal! You've
been flying round her long enough. I knew it
would come at last. So, she's got you, has she!
Well, well, Jennie's a fine girl, my boy; I danced
at her father's and mother's wedding. I wish
I had more to give you. You'll have to be content
with the lower plantation, and a dozen slaves to
start with."

"Listen, father," John urged, stopping him
with a gentle pressure on his arm. "And try to
remember. Have you encountered Butler lately?"

"Change our butler!—what better butler do

you want than Alfred? He's an aristocrat to his finger tips. I wouldn't think of reducing him from his present rank; what has he done to offend any one?"

"I mean the Judge who took the house—I mean Judge Butler."

"Ah! A man of low origin and no principle, my son—a renegade who betrayed his people for thirty pieces of silver—silver stained with blood— a dirty, contemptible office-seeker. I wouldn't lower myself by speaking to such a man."

"Yes, I know father," John broke in, "but I'm trying to recall to your memory the visits you have made at night lately to the old home."

"Of course, I love the old home. I was born here. I brought my bride here. I'll never leave it except for a better world."

John felt a lump rise in his throat and rose to go. It was useless. Besides, the thing was unthinkable. How could this feeble old man spring on one of Butler's physique and stab him to death. He couldn't, except in a moment of superhuman frenzy which sometimes comes to the insane. There was the thought which returned again and again to torment him! Aunt Julie Ann declared the ghost was seen to pass through the hall and go upstairs but a few moments before the tragedy. Yes, it was possible.

John peered into his father's restless eyes with a mad desire to lift the mysterious veil that obscured the world from his vision. The horror of the sickening tragedy strangled him and he turned, abruptly leaving the room.

He sought Billy with a growing sense of helpless and bitter despair. Since the day of their brief quarrel which followed the demonstration before old Larkin, Billy had avoided John. Since Butler's death they had scarcely spoken. The effect of this tragedy on his headstrong younger brother first led John to suspect his membership in the newly organised Klan under Steve's leadership.

John found him in his room reading.

"Billy, I must have a serious talk with you," the older brother began.

"All right, sit down," the boy answered, laying aside his book.

"A youngster of eighteen who keeps to his room for days at a time and reads is either sick or has something on his mind."

"Which do you think?" Billy asked, looking vaguely out the window.

"I'll answer you by asking a question, and I want you to answer on the honour of a Graham. Are you a member of Steve Hoyle's Klan?"

"You have no right to ask that question," was the hot reply.

"Yes, I have," John slowly said, "for two reasons. As the organiser of the original Ku Klux Klan in this state I hold myself in a measure responsible for its existence even in its lowest forms. But that's not all, my boy, you're my brother, and I love you."

Billy's eyes blinked and he looked at the ceiling. He had never heard such an expression from John's lips before.

"I wish I'd slipped my arm around you and told you that long ago. I've always been proud of your high-strung, sensitive spirit, proud in my own heart that we were of the same blood, and I want to ask you to forgive me for seeing so little of you and being of so little help to you."

A sob caught the boy's breath.

"You'll let me help you now?" John asked tenderly, extending his hand.

Billy rose trembling, his eyes running over with tears, took a step toward the door, turned and threw himself into John's arms, sobbing bitterly.

The older brother held him close for a moment in silence, and slowly said at last:

"Now tell me."

"I was at Judge Butler's that night!"

John sank to a chair with a groan.

"My God! I knew it!"

"But, of course, you know that I had nothing

to do with any attack on a man in whose house I was a guest," he went on rapidly. "The whole thing is a horrible mystery to us all. Every man in our crowd was in the ballroom dancing."

"How did you know that?" John interrupted sharply.

"Because I counted them as they entered."

"*You* counted them?"

"Yes."

"Then you were in command of the crowd?"

Billy hesitated a moment, and said:

"Yes!"

John drew a deep breath and turned his head away in anguish.

"I could not resist the temptation to lead them. I wanted to see inside the old house again—you understand. I never dreamed of anything happening."

"None of the boys were drinking?"

"No, and there wasn't a fool among them— they were all my chums and friends in town."

"Then go at once and tell them that I say to put a thousand miles between them and this town in the next forty-eight hours—to Texas if possible."

"Why?" asked Billy with a touch of wounded pride.

"There are a hundred reasons—one is enough.

There's a price on the head of the man who committed that crime."

"My men didn't do it!"

"Granted. But one of these fine days a white-livered traitor may crawl from your Klan and claim his reward of gold or office. You will be convicted in ten minutes."

Billy turned pale, and straightened his boyish figure.

"Well, I'll tell my men to go. I'll not run."

"You can serve your men best by going. The bravest general always knows when to retreat."

"I'll stand my ground."

"You must go. I can fight for you better with a thousand miles between us. I'll play a trick on my Yankee friends this time. I'm going to send you North into the enemy's country—to college."

Billy was trembling now with a new excitement. His heart was set on a college career and he hadn't as yet hoped to find the way.

"How will you do it?" he asked eagerly.

"Old Nickaroshinski will take my note. I'll borrow the money."

The boy smiled for the first time in a month.

"Oh! John, you've taken a load off my soul."

John's hand crushed the letter from Stella, which he was unconsciously grasping in his pocket.

"And you've piled one on my soul under which I'll stagger to the grave," he cried within, outwardly answering with a smile and warm grip of the hand as he said:

"Quick now, boy. Don't lose a minute. There will be some heart-broken mothers in town tomorrow night. There's but one choice: the plains of the West, or a prison pen."

"I'll go at once," Billy cried, seizing his hat and hastily leaving.

Pale and haggard, John slowly returned to his office. He looked at his watch. It was five minutes to three. Stella was waiting to receive him. He could hear the low sweet tones of her voice greeting him, and see her great brown eyes smiling their welcome.

But his mind was made up. Safety lay in flight. He wrote a brief reply to her letter.

My dear Miss Butler:

I thank you for the honour you do me in the request you make. I regret that I cannot see my way clear at present to accept your offer. I have many reasons, and I beg you to believe that they are very serious ones—otherwise I would hasten to answer in person your call.

With sincere regrets,

John Graham.

Stella received the note with mingled surprise and rage, and immediately wired the Attorney

General in the cipher code he had given her asking for the assistance for two months of the best detective the Secret Service could command. General Champion replied within two hours. "Mr. Ackerman leaves here to-night. He will report to you in Independence to-morrow."

CHAPTER IV

ACKERMAN SECURES A PLEDGE

ACKERMAN sent to Stella his letter of introduction from the Attorney General, stating that he would call the following day and report progress.

General Champion's letter had raised the highest hopes by the declaration that the young detective had developed a well defined and intelligent theory on which to conduct the prosecution of the case.

Stella awaited his call impatiently. She had pictured the ideal detective of romance and could not conceal her amazement at his personal appearance when she extended her hand to greet him.

His voice was soft and low as her own, his face wreathed in smiles—and such a face!—plump, rosy cheeked, young, fresh and boyish, save for the slightest touch of gray in the dark hair about his temples. His eye alone, to the close student of men, might have revealed his profession. It looked a steady blaze of light from beneath straight intellectual brows.

"You had better understand at once, Miss Butler," he began, "that I am a prosperous young business man from the North at present engaged in the organisation of cotton mills in the South."

Stella could not repress a smile, as she said:
·"I must say you look the part."

"I have engaged board at Mrs. Wilson's and asked Mr. John Graham to act as my attorney in the organisation of a company in this county."

"I see," she cried, for the first time catching the steady light of Ackerman's eye.

"I cannot be seen in conference with you. We will report to each other by letter. But we must clearly understand each other. Am I right that you mean to press this case to the bitter end, let the blow fall on whom it may?"

"Certainly," was the firm answer.

"I learn from the Attorney General's office that you are on the track of the man who is Commander-in-chief of the Klan in this state?"

"Yes."

"Pardon another question. I must know if you are in dead earnest? I have found that women have little tenacity of purpose in such cases and as a rule cannot be depended on."

"I'll show you that they are not all alike!" Stella broke in angrily.

"Then may I ask that if you succeed in securing this name that you will place it in my hands without a moment's delay?"

"At once."

CHAPTER V

IN THE TOILS

STELLA determined to make one more direct appeal to John Graham before resorting to indirect subterfuges for the purpose of meeting him.

She wrote half a dozen letters and tore them up. They lacked simplicity. The only effective appeal to this man must disarm all suspicion of subtlety. It must be natural, sincere and ring true. She found it a very difficult thing to express in cold written words one thing and mean another, and yet preserve the ring of truth and sincerity. At last she wrote a letter which seemed to be effective. She read it over and over, and added to the paper the faintest touch of delicate perfume, an old extract of sweet pinks, which she had used the night of their meeting. She laid it aside and waited an hour to carefully read it again. It was too important to risk a failure. Should he once suspect an ulterior purpose of any kind her plan must end in utter defeat. She spent an hour walking through the lawn, returned and read again the letter.

It seemed cold, stiff and artificial, and the touch of perfume obvious and vulgar. It lacked the magnetism of personality. She had no power to convey this as yet in words. She must see him face to face, hold him with the deep charm of her great eyes, and enfold him with the spell of her beauty.

"I must see him," she cried—"or I'll fail! If I can only touch his hand, stand by his side and look into his face, I'll win."

She walked to the window and stood thoughtful a moment. Suddenly her eyes lighted.

"I'll do it! I'll go to his dingy office and ask for his services as any other client. Why not? His sign is a standing invitation to the world. How stupid of me to be wasting paper!"

In five minutes she was on the way. Her dress was a simple girlish pattern of green dimity. A quaint bonnet of the period, flaring wide and high in front, its tiny circular crown tilted, with ribbon tied under her dainty chin, made a picture no artist could pass without a sigh.

She stopped before the wrought-iron weather-beaten sign which hung from the doorway leading up a flight of stairs to the young lawyer's office. Her heart fluttered with a moment of uncertainty as she felt herself standing on the threshold of the most daring step of her life. The plain gold letters of the sign held her with a strange fascination:

JOHN GRAHAM
ATTORNEY AND COUNSELLOR
AT LAW

She had never noticed this piece of plain black iron before, and yet somehow it seemed a part of the record of her deep inner life, and, as it moved, gently stirred by the soft breezes of a Southern day, creaking on the rod from which it hung, the sound thrilled her with a feeling of strange terror. She turned quickly away, her heart pounding with excitement, and began to retrace her steps.

She walked a block, stopped, flushed red, frowned and turned on her heels.

"I'll not be a silly coward. I'll not look back again until it's done."

This time she walked firmly up the stairs and gently knocked on his door.

John had just finished his business with Nickaroshinski. The old Jew had accepted his personal note unsecured by any endorsement for the money needed to send Billy north to college. He sat in brooding silence, idly holding between his fingers the paper on which he had recorded the memorandum of his new indebtedness. He was not worrying over his ability to pay—of that he felt sure. Butler had answered his suit by removing the order of his disbarment on Larkin's advice the day of the County Convention. His practice gave promise of a comfortable living.

It was Billy's flight, which was arranged for the following day, that had focussed his thoughts on the miserable tragedy which had raised still another barrier between him and his possible approach to Stella.

The knock on his door had not interrupted the train of his thought. He was looking through his window into the deep blue of the infinite skies, and linking in fancy the mysteries of their changing lights to those which flashed from the fathomless depths of the eyes of the woman he loved.

He had mechanically answered the knock without moving and still sat wide-eyed and dreaming when the rustle of Stella's dress and the echo of her soft footfall startled him.

He turned in amazement, stared, suddenly sprang to his feet, his face flushed with excitement. Surely he was asleep—dreaming! Or had the picture in his soul suddenly stepped from the infinite into the flesh and blood of the finite in answer to the yearning call of his heart! A hundred wild thoughts swept his imagination in the brief moment before he could speak.

"I fear I've startled you!" she said, drawing back with a timid gesture.

"Why, why—it's you—Miss Butler! I hadn't dreamed of seeing you in this dingy office!"

He stammered and hesitated, and continued to gaze at her in confusion.

"May I sit down?" she asked softly.

"I beg a thousand pardons," he answered, springing across the room for a chair. He dumped a pile of law books from it—brushed the dust from the bottom and placed it before her.

"Believe me," he went on, "I was so astonished at seeing you, I thought I must have fallen asleep —you see it was too beautiful to be true—I thought it must be a dream."

"Well, there was nothing left but to humble myself and call on you—you refused to call on me."

"I can never tell you how sorry I was to have to write that note," he said gravely.

"I'm glad, for I refuse to take your letter as final. You said there were many and serious reasons why you could not act as my counsel. I've come to hear them."

"I assure you they are serious enough, Miss Butler. I fear it will not be possible for me to state them."

"Then I refuse to accept them," she answered with a smile.

John gazed at her, wondering if she could know

what havoc her sweet appealing smile was playing with his resolutions.

He tried to speak and couldn't.

Stella continued, her voice low and musical with childlike tenderness:

"I know that my father was your political foe, but he had the profoundest respect for your ability and your high sense of honour. His death will doubtless remain one of the unexplained tragedies of the troubles through which the country is now passing."

She rose and slowly approached John's chair, her great brown eyes blinding him with their light as she gently laid a white hand on his shoulder.

He started at her touch.

"Mr. Graham," she said, with exquisite tenderness, "life is too short to cherish its bitter feuds."

"Yes," he answered in a whisper barely audible.

"I am utterly alone and distressed over business affairs I do not understand. I have implicit faith in you. I need your help and advice. Will you refuse me what you would grant without question to a stranger who would call at this office and ask?"

John flushed and fumbled his hands nervously.

"Come, you will accept, will you not?" She extended her hand. "Shall we be friends?"

He trembled for a moment and his own hand resistlessly sought hers.

"Yes!" he cried with deep emotion, unconsciously crushing her hand in his.

"You will come to-morrow morning to the house and go over the papers with me?"

"To-morrow afternoon," he replied, as a momentary cloud shadowed his brow. "I have an important engagement for the morning." And he thought of Billy with a pang.

"Then to-morrow afternoon," she cried, with a tender smile that lingered as a caress long after she had passed from the door.

CHAPTER VI

THE TRAIN FOR THE NORTH

ONE by one the boys engaged in the masquerade at the Judge's the night of his death slipped out of Independence from various nearby stations and left for the West. An hour before the time for Billy's train going North John went to his room for a chat before saying good-bye.

Billy had begun to unpack his trunk.

John seized his arm.

"What's this—what's the matter?"

"I'm not going!" he snapped.

"Why not?"

"I've found out that you may be put on trial for your life."

"Well, what's that got to do with your education?"

"You're just packing me off to get me out of danger."

"Suppose I am?"

"I'm not going to sneak out of trouble and leave you to stand for what I've done."

"I'm responsible, my boy."

"You're not. You tried to keep me out of it.

I got Steve Hoyle to take me in.   I knew what I was doing.   I was a headstrong fool."

"Because you've been a fool is no reason why you should keep it up.   Don't talk any more nonsense.   Hurry—put your clothes back in that trunk—you must catch this train."

"No!" was the dogged answer.

John put his hand on the boy's shoulder.

"You must do it for me, Billy.   I'm trying to make good my failure.   I ought to have been both father and mother to you.   I was neither—I didn't know how—forgive me! I let you slip away. It seems to me now it would have been very easy for me to have taken you by the hand, and with a jolly word or two and a little pains and a little friendly comradeship, I could have kept you out of trouble.   I'm heartsick over it, boy.   You must let me atone in this way.   You can do no good by staying.   You'll be in the way when trouble comes. You'll promise me now, because I ask you—won't you?"

The boy choked back a sob.

"I'll go on one condition——"

"Well?"

"If you get in trouble about this thing, that you'll let me know."

John grasped his hand:

"I promise you."

Mrs. Wilson and Susie accompanied them to the station. As the train signalled to pull out Billy shook hands with Susie awkwardly and tried to take leave of her mother in the same way, but Mrs. Wilson broke down, threw her arms around his neck and sobbed:

"Billy, darling, you're my own sweet boy—I love you—I love you! You'll write to me every week—won't you?"

Billy promised, disengaging himself in evident embarrassment and trying to hide his tears.

Moved by a sudden impulse Susie smiled, drew Billy's head down and kissed him.

"For the high honour you once paid me. I shall expect great things of you, Billy."

As the train started, he gripped John's hand: "Remember, we stand together. We are Grahams—I'll hold you to your promise!"

John saw Ackerman join Susie and caught the sudden flash of his keen eye.

He touched his lip in sign of warning to Billy and waved his hand:

"I'll remember! Good luck!"

CHAPTER VII

THE DAUGHTER OF EVE

STELLA had piled on the big oblong oak table in the library the letters and legal documents relating to her father's estate.

She had determined to treat John Graham's first visit as a purely business one, and make her approach to him by the more subtle way of child-like dependence on his help and advice.

She wore on purpose the same simple green dimity dress in which she had called at his office. Each step in her plans must be taken with the utmost care. He had masked his feelings with an iron will and she could as yet form no conception of the impression she had made.

Seated beside the table, idly turning the papers, she awaited his coming to-night with the keenest interest, every faculty of her being keyed to the highest pitch of power.

A letter from Ackerman had aroused anew her curiosity over every detail of the murder of her father and had given her a definite purpose toward which to work during John's visit. She

studied carefully again the paragraph in which
he said:

"I have made several important discoveries in the past
twenty-four hours. (1) That old Isaac has left the county
and is not holding a sanctification meeting as he told his
wife. (2) That Larkin and your father had a violent
quarrel on the day of the Convention. (3) That a dozen
young men, one at a time, have left Independence recently.
(4) And most important, that the tradition that there is
a secret passage somewhere into the Graham house must
be true. If you can confirm this fourth fact for me by its
discovery my work will be greatly helped."

Stella had quietly ransacked the house from
cellar to attic in vain searching for this secret way.
She had questioned Aunt Julie Ann without results,
and had made up her mind to gain from John first
this important fact.

The brass knocker struck three sharp strokes on
the front door. With a quick, cat-like movement
she concealed Ackerman's letter in her bosom,
smoothed her dress, and as the young lawyer
entered, rose and greeted him with a gracious smile.

"I must thank you again for undertaking this
work for me," she said, taking his hand. "It
is such a relief to feel that it is now in the hands
of one who understands—one I can trust
implicitly."

"It will be a pleasure if I can serve you," he
answered gravely.

"I have the papers all spread out here ready for you."

"Pardon me, if I look about the room a moment," John said with deep emotion. "You see I haven't been in this room before for years. I spent many happy hours in it, in the old days."

"I hope this will not be the last time you will enter, now that we are going to be friends. When we have time you must take me all through in every nook and corner—show me all the secret closets and dark passageways and tell me its history."

"Yes, of course"—he answered with an absent look.

"I don't believe you were listening to what I said at all," she exclaimed with mock anger. "A penny for your real thoughts!"

"May I be bold enough to tell you just what I was thinking?"

"Yes."

"I was thinking," he said with a sober smile, "what a beautiful picture you make in this old oak panelled room. The delicate lines of your face seem at home here as though the master workman who carved the figure in that mantel had seen you in a vision while he was at work."

"What a dreamer you are!" she laughed.

"And you are willing to trust me as a lawyer?"

"Absolutely."

"Then I must prove myself worthy, mustn't I?"

"The papers are ready"—she said, bustling about the table and mixing the bundles in greater confusion with an attempt at arranging them in business order.

John seated himself and began to examine them. She bent over his shoulder saying with a light laugh:

"I'll do my best to explain them—they are all Greek to me—but you'll understand."

"I'm sure there will be no great difficulty."

He ran rapidly over the bundles and in half an hour had made memorandums of each division of the work before him. He took up one of the packages and began its careful reading, but the writing faded. He could hear Stella softly breathing as she bent near him and see the beautiful little hand resting on the table. He was seized with a mad impulse to grasp it and clasp her in his arms. He smiled and placed his hand on his forehead a moment lest she might see his confusion. He could endure it no longer. He must leave and regain control of himself.

He tied the packages of papers together and rose.

"You are going so soon?" she asked.

"Yes, I'll take them down to my office. It will require several hours to go over them."

"You will come again to-morrow?" she said softly.

"I'll report to you again to-morrow evening."

"I shall expect you at eight," she said, extending her hand.

He held it unconsciously for an instant, and wondered if she could feel the pounding of his heart.

He came each evening for a week and spent two hours in the library with Stella until every letter and paper had been thoroughly examined. In a hundred little ways she had made him feel the power and charm of her personality; in no way so keenly, perhaps, as in the long silences during which she sat near with her great brown eyes watching him intently. He could feel their deep mysterious light in whatever direction he turned. In no other way could she have made so powerful an appeal to his imagination. To his poetic fancy, this capacity for silent comradeship in a girl so young revealed a depth of character which he had not suspected.

The real depth of its meaning he could not dream. The moments of exultant triumph, of breathless suspense, of merciless cruelty with which she watched him slowly entering the trap she had set, were safely concealed beneath the childlike expression of her beautiful face.

Each night he felt his resolution to allow no word of love to pass his lips harder and harder to keep. And each night she watched with increasing excitement his gradual approach to the brink of the precipice to which she silently beckoned.

On the night of his final report when the work was finished, she looked at him intently and said:

"Now, I'm going to hold you to your promise."

"And have I broken one?"

"Only forgotten it, I think—you must go over the old house with me—every nook and corner. But before we start, come, you are tired, I've some refreshments for you."

She led the way into the dining room where she had prepared a dainty supper. Aunt Julie Ann in spotless white cap and apron, stood smiling her welcome. The table was lighted with a dozen wax candles set in two old silver candelabra which had belonged to the Graham family more than a hundred years, until they had fallen with the house and its furnishings into the Judge's hands.

Stella seated herself at one end of the table which had been shortened to its smallest size and placed John at the other. Her position, the lights and the effects of the picture in his imagination, she had carefully planned and rehearsed before his arrival. She meant to win to-night.

Behind her stood the rich old mahogany sideboard of Colonial pattern, the Graham silver flashing in the quaint gold mirror which hung above it. In the mirror her own image was clearly reflected. The man opposite could look into her face and at the same time see in the shining silvery picture above the sideboard the black ringlets of curling hair at the back of her neck, as well as the exquisite lines of her figure.

John gazed at her in silent wonder. Never had he seen a picture so appealing in its beauty to every sense of his being. He felt that she was born to sit at that table amid such surroundings.

She lifted the teapot to fill his cup:

"This little feast is to celebrate the completion of our work."

"And seal our friendship, may I hope?" he broke in with a smile.

"Yes," she answered in a whisper.

These soft notes of her voice thrilled the man before her, and his whole being quivered in response to their call. He wondered if he could conceal the hunger with which he was looking into her eyes.

He had always thought her the most beautiful being he had ever seen, but to-night for the first time she had dressed specially to receive him, and his imagination had not dreamed the picture—Her beauty fairly stunned him.

Her dress was of filmy zephyr-like white chiffon, cut low to show the full lines of the neck and shoulders. Around the upper part of her beautiful bare arms, where they melted into the shoulders, was drawn a scarf of delicate lace. Where it crossed the waist line in V shape, was pinned an ivorytype miniature portrait of her proud mother, painted at her own age of twenty, which looked so strikingly like the living form above, it might have been taken for the image of a twin sister. A sash of pink ribbon encircled her figure. The skirt hung in full puffy lines draped over a number of under-skirts after the fashion of the period. The bottom of the skirt was finished with a border of lace on the top of which were set at intervals clusters of little pink roses wrought in silk.

Her curly crown of black hair was parted in the middle and drawn low on the side of the face in two great waves and tied behind with a pink ribbon. The long ends were curled into four strands and thrown carelessly around her neck in front and hung to the waist. Her head was circled with a tiny wreath of the living pink roses from which the silk ones had been modelled. To John's fancy this wreath against her black hair seemed the jewelled crown of a queen set in priceless rubies.

She poured the tea with her bare arm uplifted

in a fascinating pose, the right arm curved just
enough to tilt the teapot and yet preserve the dimple
at her elbow. In all his life he could not remember an arm like these—so graceful, so seductive
each little movement, they seemed to possess a
conscious soul of their own. Her whole being
spoke the charm of the boundless vitality of youth
just budding into perfect womanhood. Her delicate skin flashed its tints in harmony with every
mood of thought in her voice. She had as a
divine gift a sensitiveness of expression, so acute
that it could be controlled by the fierce will which
hid beneath the velvet surface. She could blush
at will because her imagination was so vivid that
she could direct its powers by a subtle process of
auto-suggestion.

John had not realised until he saw her eat how
wonderful were the lines of her luscious lips. He
felt that he could sit there forever and watch her
dainty wrist and tapering fingers lift the cup.
Her eyes were friendly to-night! They looked at
him with dreamy tenderness, a childlike trust, and
perfect faith.

How could he live through the evening without
telling her of his love! Yet he must keep silent.
He felt with deep foreboding an approaching
catastrophe which must soon overwhelm the men
who had created an Empire whose power they

could not control. That Empire had left a stain of blood on the floor of this house—a stain that must forever darken his own life and hers—and yet—how could he give her up?

He rose from the table at her suggestion and followed her in a spell as she lifted a silver candlestick above her head and started to explore the house.

He found his tongue at last and told her with boyish enthusiasm the legends of the old mansion, the associations of each room, and sketched with good-humoured criticism the peculiarities of his people. In the gallery of the observatory he showed her the spots from which the slightest sounds were echoed to the hall below, and explained the origin of many of the ghost stories which the Negroes believed with such implicit faith.

Stella leaned over the railing and looked down into the hall at the chair in which her father had fallen the night of the dance, and a curious smile played about her lips.

"And what are you smiling at?" he asked softly.

Without the quiver of an eyelid, either in surprise or recognition of the fact that he had caught her in a moment off her guard, she replied:

"I was just wondering if you ever believed in ghosts?"

"Of course," he laughed.

"Really?"

"Yes. When Aunt Julie Ann used to tell them to me at night in the nursery they were vivid and terrible realities."

"And you've laughed away all the romances of childhood now?"

"No," he answered firmly. "I halfway believe in ghosts still, and the old dreams of beauty and love, of honour and truth, seem to me more and more the only things in human life that have any value."

They had returned to the hall. Stella placed the candle on the table and sat down on the davenport. John followed her instinctively and seated himself by her side.

Suddenly she placed her soft hand on his, exclaiming:

"Oh! There's one thing we've forgotten!" She felt him tremble at her touch.

"What?"

"The legend of the secret way—tell me about it—how it originated and all—of course, I know it is only a legend. Such things are only found in stories."

John looked at her, with a smile playing about the corners of his mouth.

"You have ceased to believe in romance, ghosts and fairies?"

"I'll believe it if you tell me," she said softly.

John took her hand and lifted her from the lounge.

"Have you faith enough to follow me through the dark secret way to-night if I can find it for you?"

"Yes!" she whispered, leaning toward him trustingly.

"Then I'm going to do what was never done before—show this secret way to one who does not answer to the name of Graham."

Stella's bosom rose and fell with deep emotion as she turned her brown eyes on John.

"But why not?" he continued. "The house is yours. And I'm haunted with the strange fancy that your spirit has lived here before."

"I have grown to love it," she said hesitatingly, "in spite of the tragedy. It's strange. I wonder at myself for it."

John turned toward the panel in the wainscoting whose location he knew so well, paused and said:

"I'd better wait and let you change your dress. You'll soil it against the damp narrow walls."

Stella's eyes were sparkling now with excitement.

"No matter. I can't wait a minute. The mystery and romance will be worth a dress. Show me the way. I'll follow."

"All right," John answered, as he extended

his hand and pressed the moulding behind which
lay the spring. The panel flew open and a rush
of cool air took Stella's breath.

"Heavens!" she exclaimed, clinging suddenly
to John's arm, "why, I had no idea it could open
here just behind us in the hall!"

He could feel her tremble.

"There's not the slightest danger—you need not
be afraid," he said, tenderly. "Wait, I'll get
the candle and go before you."

He took the candle from the centre table and
entered the passage-way, closing the panel.

"Wait, you must hold my hand," Stella cried
timidly.

He took the soft little hand in his with a throb
of joy and carefully led her down the tiny stairs
into the basement, where the passage turned
between two walls and again descended a half
dozen steps to another door which led out of the
house into the long straight way to the vault.

Trembling with excitement, she clung in silence
to his hand as they entered the long damp passage.
He closed the door suddenly, the sound crashing
through the narrow walls in a thousand startling
echoes.

Stella sprang into his arms, nestling close and
whispered:

"Mercy! what was that?"

"Only the door," he laughed.

"It scared me nearly to death," she faltered, slowly withdrawing from his sheltering protection while she skilfully managed to press her soft bare arm against his hand. She felt him tremble, his breath deepen and quicken at the touch of her flesh.

"You're sure there's no danger?" she asked.

"Not the slightest," he replied cheerily. "Just one more little surprise and we are out in the moonlight on the lawn."

He led her clinging to his hand along the dark way, holding the flickering candle above her head, a hundred mad impulses of love surging through his brain.

They stopped at the stoneset door leading into the tomb, and he handed her the candle, gently disengaging his other hand. He drew the heavy door back, Stella stepped through and he followed close behind her.

She raised the candle high and looked about the vault. With a sudden cry, she staggered into his arms gasping:

Why,—we're—in—the—vault!"

The candle dropped from her hand and she threw her arm around John's neck clinging to him frantically. Her hold relaxed and her head drooped against his breast. He clasped her tenderly for a moment and his lips instinctively touched the curling mass of her hair, as he cried in agony:

"God help me—I'm lost!"

She revived as quickly as she had collapsed and murmured:

"I was about to faint—quick, let's get out!"

He led her through the iron grilled door into the moonlit shadows of the lawn.

"Oh!" she cried with a gasp of relief. "What a wild experience! I hope I didn't do anything very silly—did I?" she asked dreamily.

"You did just what any little girl of your age might do under such conditions," he replied, gazing at her with deep seriousness. "Come, let us find a seat on the lawn and I'll tell you the story of the vault and the secret way."

He led her to the seat on which he had sunk in despair the night he came half-mad with pain to watch the masqueraders whirl past her lighted windows.

The full moon wrapped the earth in the white mantle of Southern midsummer glory, and the night wind stirred, its breath laden with the rich perfume of every flower in full bloom. A katydid was singing a plaintive song in the tree above, and in the rose bushes near the porch a mocking-bird rehearsed in a burst of mad joy every love song of the feathered world.

In low, rapid tones John told her the story of
Robert Graham's great love for his Huguenot
grandmother and why he built the vault and
secret way. She listened and furtively watched him struggling with his emotions. Suddenly he turned, looked tenderly into her
eyes and took her hand.

"After all, Miss Stella, what else matters on
earth, when life has once been made glorious by
a great, deathless love—such a love as that which
has grown in my own heart for you."

Stella turned away to hide the flash of triumph
with which her face was flushed.

"Ah! don't answer me now," he rushed on.
"I don't ask it. I only beg the privilege of telling
you—telling you how you have lifted my soul from
the shadows of self and hate, and made life
radiant and beautiful. I dare not hope that you
love me yet—that you only hear me is enough.
That I sit by your side and tell you is all I ask.
My love is so deep, so full, so rich, so great, it is
glory and life and strength within itself. I could
die to-night and count my life a triumph, because
I've seen you and loved you, and you have heard
me. May I tell you all that is in my heart?"

He leaned closer and pressed her hand gently.

"Yes," she whispered. "Why not?"

"I dare not tell you why I pause to ask the question. I've sometimes thought that an impassable gulf yawned between us. To-night I've thrown such rubbish to the winds. There's no gulf so wide, so deep and dark the heart of love may not leap it. Nothing matters save that I love you, that you smile and hear me!"

"I am honoured in your love," she answered gently.

"Ah! you can never know how sweet it is to hear that from your dear lips. I cannot tell you the madness of the joy that fills me, when I realise that I have found in you all I've ever dreamed of beauty, tenderness and purity. All the songs of life that poets dream and find no words in which to sing, I feel within. If you should send me from your presence now, I'd laugh at Death for I have tasted Life! To win your love is all I ask of this world or the next—You will let me try?"

"Yes," said the low voice, as she placed her hand again in his.

"Then I must go," he said, rising and lifting her from the seat—"I've said enough to-night. I must go before I dare say too much and break the spell of joy that holds me."

At the door he asked.

"I may come again to-morrow?"

"Yes, at eight."

He bowed and kissed the tips of her fingers.

"I may have something to say to you to-morrow," she said seriously.

"I shall count the minutes of every hour that separates us."

She watched the tall figure pass swiftly and joyously along the white gravelled moonlit walk, while a pæan of fierce joy welled within her heart.

"I've won—I've won, beyond the shadow of a doubt!" she cried, exultantly.

CHAPTER VIII

THE TRACKS AT THE DOOR

WITHIN thirty minutes after Ackerman had received Stella's message that she had found the secret entrance to the house he was waiting for her at the door of the vault as she had suggested.

He had entered by the rear wagon road and passed into the shrubbery without attracting the attention of the servants.

She showed him the way to the underground passage through the niche in the rear of the vault, and in ten minutes Ackerman entered the hall through the panel under the stairs.

Stella, who had returned to the house across the lawn, watched the panel slowly open at his touch and her eyes gleamed with a cold, hard light as she saw reënacted in imagination the tragedy of her father's death.

The detective made an accurate diagram of the hall, measured carefully the distance of the secret door from the chair in which the Judge had been found, and reëxamined the ballroom and all its possible exits and entrances.

Stella returned to the entrance of the vault and placed a padlock and chain on its iron door while Ackerman again entered the underground passage and spent two hours alone, making the most minute examinations and measurements of every track to be found at any point from the door of the vault to the panel in the wainscoting. The work of measurement was rendered easy by the accumulation of soft earth in the bottom of the underground way from the action of the water which had soaked through the brick ceiling and walls.

He discovered the footprints of eleven different men besides the dainty mark of Stella's little shoe made the night before.

He returned to the hall and asked her permission to come from time to time and continue his study of the grounds.

"Certainly," she answered eagerly. "And your discoveries?"

"Confirm so far my theory of the crime," he answered quickly. "The assassins undoubtedly entered the house by this secret passage, committed the crime and passed quickly out without discovery. I did not know who was with you last night, but he has been there at least once before within the past few weeks."

"Is it possible!" Stella exclaimed.

"I find," he continued, "that he merely took

a single step inside the door leading from the vault into the underground passage as if he were showing the way to others who traversed the entire length."

Stella's red lips were suddenly pressed tight and Ackerman watched her keenly.

"This may mean something or it may mean nothing. It all depends on what night he stepped inside the door."

"I see," she said cautiously.

"Other facts I have found are of significance," he went on. "I have located Mr. Isaac A. Postle, and learned from him two startling things. First that he encountered John Graham at the gate on the night of the murder—collided with him, he declares, as he was running from the masked men who had just galloped past his cottage."

The girl smothered a cry.

"He also says that later in the evening, just before the murder occurred, he passed by the front door and saw John Graham seated on a rustic bench in the shadows watching the house."

"It's horrible—it's horrible!" Stella murmured.

"The two statements contradict each other. Uncle Isaac is lying at some point of his story. If he ran for his life from the masqueraders he certainly would not have returned to the house in thirty minutes while they were still there. Until

I can find the motive for that lie his story must be taken with a large grain of salt. In the meantime if you can confirm for me his statement that Graham was here on that night you will do me a service."

"Within a week I'll tell you," she replied, the strange cold light flashing again from her eyes.

CHAPTER IX

A TEST OF STRENGTH

IN TAKING leave of Ackerman Stella went
immediately to her room to select her dress
and plan her campaign for John Graham's
reception in the evening.

A feeling of reaction depressed her. The
passionate warmth and tenderness of his love
remained a haunting memory. A sense of loneliness crept into her heart. She began to see that
she was playing a desperate game with the great
stake of a human life as the issue. The consciousness of its possible tragedy began to be
dimly felt. She sat staring idly at the gowns she
had piled on the big tester bed without being
able to make a selection.

"I've begun a daring task," she mused. "The
wit and beauty of a girl of twenty against the iron
will and personality of a man of genius. A man
just entering his thirtieth year, who has looked
Death in the face on the field of battle and
dared defy the power of the Government that
has crushed him. Can I win?"

The closer she had drawn to John Graham in

their intimate daily association the more impossible seemed the idea that such a man could have murdered her father or known of such a crime. And yet the closer each day drew the net of circumstantial evidence about him and the fiercer grew her determination to demand the life of the murderer.

What had surprised her most of all in his character was the spirit of eternal youth within him—youth strong, fresh, buoyant and throbbing with poetic ideals. At first she had thought him sombre and morose, yet in his presence she could never imagine him more than twenty years of age. In many of his little ways and moods she found him more boy than man. And she must acknowledge the truth—she had begun to think of his possible death as a criminal with a pang of regret.

She rose and studied her beautiful figure in her mirror until self and pride once more filled the universe.

"Bah! What to me is the life of the man who struck my father dead at my feet! I'll amuse myself by playing the game of love with him for a week, and then for the master-stroke. I'll watch him as a cat a mouse, and when I'm ready, strike to kill. If he had no mercy, I shall have none."

John found her in a mood of elusive girlishness. When he begged her to remember her parting words, the half-pledged promise of a message for which he waited, she only laughed and fenced.

She allowed him to call each afternoon and evening for a week until he was drunk with the joy of her presence—until the sense of personal intimacy and the growing consciousness of comradeship had made his will obedient to her slightest whim. It amused her to watch the growth of his powers of intuition, born of this daily life, which enabled him to anticipate her wishes.

For the man, these days were as water to the lips of a thirsty dreamer. In the heart of the girl, who studied his every movement with deep sinister purpose, there had grown a cruel joy in the consciousness of the tyranny she wielded over a powerful human life.

Toward the end of the week he began to beg her tenderly for a single word of love. At last she promised him an answer on the evening following, and forbade his afternoon call. She knew the effect of his longer absence would be to give her greater power. At last she was sure that the hour had struck toward which she had moved with such infinite pains, the hour of his complete surrender and his utter trust, when she had but to breathe her wish to know the guarded secrets of the Klan and they would be whispered into her ear without a moment's hesitation.

She had planned to lead him to the seat amid
the shadows of the trees near the house from which
Isaac said he had watched the dance the night of
the tragedy, and if possible gain both important
secrets at once.

She again selected the low cut white chiffon
she wore the night he had declared his love.

Maggie's keen eyes watched her dress with a
care never shown before. The little black maid
flashed her white teeth more than once behind
her back as she observed the delicate yet sure art
with which, by a touch here and there, her mistress
managed to suggest with unusual daring the
physical charms of her extraordinary beauty.
When the task was finished and she surveyed her
form in her mirror with a look of proud content,
Maggie laughed:

"You sho' is trying ter kill 'im to-night!"

"Maggie, how dare you suggest such a thing!"

"De Laws a mussy, Miss Stella, I des mean dat
you'se de purtiest thing in de whole worl' an' he
gwine drap dead quick as he sees ye!"

"That will do, Maggie," she said severely.

"Yassum."

But in spite of her severity, the mistress smiled
at the maid, and Maggie burst into a fit of laughter.
When at length it subsided, she stood with wide
staring worshipful eyes gazing at Stella entranced.

"Ef I could look lak dat, Miss Stella, I'd let 'em bile me in ile, roast me on a red-hot stove and peel me!"

"You are breaking the Ten Commandments, Maggie."

"Yassum, I'd bust a hundred commandments ef I could look lak you."

"I accept the compliment, if I can't commend your morals."

"Yassum."

A sudden flash of lightning revealed the clouds of a rapidly approaching summer storm.

Stella frowned.

"It's going to storm," she said, fretfully,

"Yassum, but he'll come."

The mistress laughed in spite of herself.

"I'm not worrying about his coming, Maggie."

"Nobum, you needn't worry. He swim er river ef he couldn't git here no odder way—dar he is now!"

His familiar knock echoed through the hall and the maid hastened to open the door.

When Stella stood before him, John seized both her hands and looked into her deep eyes with silent rapture.

"How glorious you are to-night!" he whispered passionately.

She made no answer save the sensitive smile of

triumph which lighted her face and quivered through her form.

"I meant to find a seat on the lawn to-night, but it's going to rain."

"Yes, I ran, to get here first," he cried with boyish enthusiasm—"It's raining now, but the old davenport under the stairs is cosey on a rainy night."

She looked at the panel door and hesitated.

"You're not afraid of ghosts from below I hope?" he laughed.

"No, I've locked the iron door," she announced soberly, taking her seat by his side.

With a vivid flash of lightning followed by a crash of thunder the storm broke, the big rain-drops mixed with hail rattling furiously against the windows.

Stella nestled closer to his side, and John turned his swarthy, eager face toward her.

"Now, while the storm roars," he whispered, "and shuts out the world, drawing us closer together—so close I feel that there is no world beyond the touch of your hand and the music of your voice—won't you tell me what my heart is starving to hear?"

"Do you realise what it means for a girl to say to a man, 'I love you'?" she asked slowly.

"I do," was the quick answer.

"In all its depths?"

"Yes. It means the utter surrender of soul and body or it means nothing!"

"And yet, you ask that I say it?"

"I know that I'm not worthy, but Love has always dared to claim its own, soul crying to soul, mate calling to mate—I love you! I love you! Ah! The story is old as the throb of life, yet always new and full of wonder. I know it's too much to ask, yet I dare to ask it."

"There should be no shadows between those who thus love, should there?" she asked with a far-away dreamy look as if his burning words had caught her spirit in their spell.

"No," he answered, solemnly. "A thousand times I've longed to tell you how tender was my sympathy for you in the tragedy that threw its shadow across your young life in this hall a few months ago."

"And yet you didn't," she said reproachfully, studying him keenly and furtively, with her head bowed as if in grief for the memory of her father.

"How could I without hypocrisy? The Judge and I had been uncompromising enemies. Could I tear my heart open and let the vulgar world see the deep secret of my love for you?"

"You loved me then?" she broke in with surprise.

"From the moment you crossed this old hall the night I met you."

"Loved me when you refused to answer my appeal in person the day I wrote you?"

"I refused because I loved you."

She looked at him a moment with a feeling of sudden fear. For the first time she realised with a shock that her imperious will to master his life was not the only force at work. The shadowy figure of Fate stood grim and silent before her.

"The man who wins my heart," she said firmly, "can hold no reservations—he must be all mine, body and soul. He asks as much of me. I demand the same. Are you ready to place your life in my hands as I am asked to place mine in yours?"

"Without reservation," he answered.

"I must be frank with you," she said, turning her eyes appealingly on him. "Since the awful night I saw my father sitting dead in that chair with those masked figures, white, silent and terrible behind me, I have had a morbid curiosity mingled with terror for everything and everyone connected with the Klan. I have heard that you are a member?"

John suddenly knelt before her and took her hand.

"Here on my knees before you and before God— and when I am before you I am in the presence of

God!—I call the spirit of the dead back on the wings of this storm to-night into this hall to witness when I swear to you that I am innocent of any knowledge of his death!"

"And there shall be not one shadow between us?"

"Not one. Every secret of my life shall be laid bare before I'd dare claim you as my wife. I only beg to-night one word of love from your dear lips. You believe me when I swear to you, on my honour, my life, my love that I am innocent?"

"Yes, I believe and trust you!"

He bowed and kissed her fingers reverently.

"And now you must show that you trust me before I speak," she went on dreamily—"you are in reality the Chief of the Klan in North Carolina, are you not?"

John's hand trembled, his lips quivered, and a look of mortal anguish overspread his face.

"Please don't ask me that yet?" he begged.

"You are afraid to trust me?" she said reproachfully.

"I trust you implicitly," he cried, pressing her hand, but do not ask me now!"

"The hands of Southern women made those white and scarlet costumes," she persisted. "May I not share at least one of its secrets with them?"

"Remember that conditions have changed!"

he urged—"A price is set on the head of every member of the Klan. The South now swarms with spies—the Government is straining every nerve to learn the secrets of the order—have I the right even to breathe the name of the Klan while another's life may hang on my word?"

"I see," she cried with scorn, rising. "The daughter of a murdered 'Scalawag' judge may not be trusted as other loyal women of the proud old aristocratic South!"

"Please, I beg of you——"

"You may go!" she said proudly.

And without another word she quickly turned, ascended the stairs and disappeared.

John stood for a moment blind and dumb with pain, mechanically took his hat and slowly passed through the door and out into the black, raging storm.

CHAPTER X

BEHIND BOLTED DOORS

JOHN GRAHAM fought his way home heedless of the storm's blinding fury. The hurricane without was but a zephyr to the one which raged within his own soul. Again and again he asked himself the question why Stella should have demanded of him such a confession.

He had instantly resented it. Perhaps he had scented danger. And yet it was preposterous to think the girl he worshipped could have desired this dangerous knowledge to be used against him.

Ackerman in discussing his mill projects in the office during the afternoon had asked him a number of irritating questions about the Klan which he had skilfully parried. His mind was over-sensitive and sore perhaps from this annoyance. Ackerman could have nothing to do with Stella— they were not even passing acquaintances.

From every point of view he tested the problem of her possible design to use this knowledge and found it preposterous. There was but one reasonable explanation. She had found with her keen woman's intuition the one weak spot in his mental attitude toward her. Yes, it was true. He loved her with passionate devotion, but he had not fully trusted her. She had discovered it. Had she not thus revealed the true state of her own heart? She must love him. Otherwise this keen sensitiveness to his moods would not be possible. The thought was sweet in spite of his agony over their break. After all she was right, proud little queen of his heart, to demand his loyal faith! Should he yield to her this perilous secret of his own life? Would he thus endanger those with whom he had been associated in the daring task of saving the civilisation of the South in the blackest hour of her history?

While the battle thus raged in his soul he reached his room, removed his drenched clothing and replaced them with dry ones. He walked to his window and looked out on the spluttering street lamp across the way struggling to hold its tiny flame against the storm and wondered why he had dressed again. He should have gone to bed. And then the dawning sense of loss and misery crushed him. He sank into a chair and watched the rain dash against the glass and stream down the sides of the window, his heart aching in dumb agony.

"My God!" he cried at last, "I can't live without her! She loves me, and I must win her!"

The memory of her cold words as she ordered him from the house came crashing back into his heart with sinister echoes. Never had he seen a human being so transformed by anger—eyes that a moment before had held him enraptured with their tender light had flashed cold points of steel. Hands, soft and warm and full of velvet feeling, had closed in rage as the claws of a tigress!

Suppose she refused to see him again? It was unthinkable. He seemed to have lived a century within the weeks since she had called him to her side. The life which had gone before grew dim. Four years of war and two years of daring secret revolution as a leader of the Invisible Empire faded from his consciousness. Only a great love remained, and those days by her side seemed to hold the full measure of his life.

He undressed and went to bed, only to roll and toss hour after hour without sleep.

He saw the first gray light of dawn with a sense of utter desolation. The rain had ceased an hour before. Swift flying clouds and swaying tree-tops heralded the coming of a clear, beautiful day. He determined to write at once and beg to see her. In a moment his mind was on fire with his passionate plea. As the sun rose, reflecting through scurrying clouds its scarlet and purple glory, he hastily dressed, sat down at his table and poured out his anguish in burning words of tenderness and love. He read it over with renewed hope. Never had he expressed himself so well. The letter was a living thing. No woman's hand could touch it without feeling its vital power. An immortal soul beat within it.

He had added the last line of a postscript begging her to name an early hour at which he might call, and sat in dull moody reverie unconscious of the flight of time.

A gentle knock on his door roused him. He opened it and stared blankly at Susie's gentle face.

"I trust you're not sick, Mr. John," she said. "Everybody is through breakfast. I've kept yours warm."

"Thank you, Miss Susie. I've only a little headache. I won't eat any breakfast. I've important work at the office. I'm going down at once."

As he passed her at the head of the stairs she said with a wistful look:

"Mama says she heard you stirring all night. If I can help you, won't you let me?"

"Yes, little comrade, I will. I'll let you know," he answered, swinging quickly down the stairs and out the front door.

He found a boy on the street and sent him to
Stella with his letter. He stood at his office door
and watched him until out of sight and counted
the minutes until he reappeared. He had paid
him a dime on dispatching the letter and promised
to double it if he came back in a hurry. Fifteen
minutes later he smiled as he saw the boy coming
in a run, his swift bare feet making the dirt fly
in the middle of the street.

"I knew it! Of course, she will see me!" he
exclaimed as he bounded up his stairs two rounds
at a jump. He gave the astonished boy a quarter
instead of another dime, hurried into his office,
and slammed the door. He felt the weight of the
letter with faint misgivings. It was large to have
been written so quickly. Yet it was addressed
with her own dear hand. He tore it open, and
from his trembling fingers dropped his own letter
with the seal unbroken. Not a line from her.
Her meaning could not be misunderstood. She
could have offered him no deeper insult. He sank
to his seat with a groan and sat for an hour in a
stupor of wounded pride. "I won't accept
such an answer from her!" he cried bitterly.
"And I won't stand on ceremony."

He walked down the street to the gate of the
driveway of the Graham house, hoping he might
find Aunt Julie Ann at her cottage. The door

was closed and he could get no response to his knock. He looked longingly at the old house shining with its snow white doors and windows against the dark fresh green of the rain-soaked trees, and thought with a pang of his quarrel over its possession. What did houses matter if the heart was sick unto death! The humblest Negro cabin would be a palace if only her face would shine from the doorway!

He felt himself drawn toward her with resistless force and before he realised what he was doing his hand was on the brass knocker and its echoes were ringing through the hall.

Aunt Julie Ann shook her head as she ushered him in.

"I wish ye hadn't come, marse John," she said sorrowfully.

"Why not?"

"She shut hersef up in de room an' won't let nobody come in. I creep up to de door, and hear her cryin' sof' an' low. I knock an' she didn' answer. I knock again an' calls her sweet names an' ax her please lemme do sumfin for her. She jump up an' stamp her foot an' say she kill me ef I doan' leave her 'lone. I'se skeered of her, honey, she ain't lak our folks. When de old Boy's in her lak it is ter day she talks jes lak de Judge. When she laughs an' plays an' looks purty as an angel her voice jest like her Ma's, low an' sweet."

"Tell her I'm here and wish to see her."—John interrupted with impatience.

Aunt Julie Ann shook her head again:

"You better not honey!"

"I must see her. Try!"

John stood at the foot of the stairs nervously fumbling his hat while Aunt Julie Ann climbed to the floor and knocked on her door.

He listened breathlessly for her answer. The key clicked in the lock and Stella opened it wide enough to be distinctly heard. Her voice rang cold and clear:

"Tell Mr. Graham to leave this house instantly and never enter it again!"

The door closed and the bolt flashed into its place again.

John's face flushed red, the colour slowly fading as his strong jaws snapped with new determination.

"In spite of the devil, I'll win her yet!"

CHAPTER XI

TWO days passed without a word of hope for John. On the third morning after his dismissal by Stella he sat pale and listless at breakfast, scarcely tasting his food, while Susie watched his drawn face with keen sympathetic eyes.

An hour later she entered his office.

"You promised to let me help you," she said quietly. "I have come."

He looked at her a moment and wondered why he had never before seen her striking beauty. A tall figure with exquisite sylph like lines, a serene and perfectly moulded face with straight, thoughtful brows shadowing the tenderest gray-blue eyes, and a crown of luxuriant auburn blonde hair.

He caught at once the sincere sympathy of her mood, as he pressed her hand.

"I never saw you so beautiful, Miss Susie, or your face so sweet and restful."

She blushed and looked out the window.

"I can't tell you how I thank you for coming. I think we must have been brother and sister in some other world before this."

The corners of the girl's lips twitched and she turned her tender eyes full on John's.

"You are in love with Stella?"

"Yes."

"And she has rejected you?"

"No, we have quarrelled and she refuses to see me or read my letters."

"She loves you?"

"I've hoped so, I don't know. She lets me feel it without words."

"We are friends, what can I do?"

"See her and beg her for God's sake to let me call, at least to read my letters. Will you go to-day?"

"Immediately."

"Thank you," he cried, again tenderly pressing her hand. "You must have loved too, Miss Susie."

"Perhaps I have," was the soft reply. "Write your message and I'll take it."

John seated himself and hastily wrote:

My dear Stella:

From the bottom of a heart crushed with anguish I ask your pardon for my lack of faith. Your pride was right. Give me a chance and I will show you what the trust of perfect love means for me. I await from you the words of life or death.

John Graham.

Susie promised to return at once with her answer. She knocked at the door of the old Graham house with a strange conflict raging in her own breast. She hoped to succeed for the sake of the aching heart of the man she had left, and yet mingled with the fear of failure was the half-mad wish that Stella might reject his plea.

Aunt Julie Ann's face was troubled as she greeted Susie.

"Tell Miss Stella, that I'm very sorry to learn of her illness and I trust she can see me a moment."

"Yassum, I tell her—but I'se feard she ain't well enough."

Aunt Julie Ann returned immediately, smiling.

"She say come right up to her room, Miss Susie."

Susie was shocked to note the change in the beautiful young face lying still and pale against the white pillow.

"I'm sorry to find you so ill!"

"Yes, I suppose I have nerves," she said, smiling wanly. "I didn't know it before. I think some of them must have snapped—but I'm better now. I'll get up this afternoon."

"I've something that will help you, if you will take it."

Stella's brow clouded, and her eyes, wide and cold, assumed a sinister half-mad expression.

"You have a message from Mr. Graham?"

"How did you guess it?"

"He has tried every other possible way. I wondered if he would stoop to this."

"Stoop!—what do you mean?"

"To use you for such a purpose."

"And why not?"

"You ask that of me?" The great brown eyes pierced Susie's soul.

"Certainly."

"Then it's all right," she said with a light laugh.

"You must receive his message," Susie said. "You've won the heart of the noblest man I have ever known—a great, beautiful, measureless love. Don't turn away from it—you may not know its like again."

The full lips smiled curiously.

"I've brought you a letter from him—you must read it."

Susie pressed the letter into Stella's hand and turned away to the window. She heard the rattle of the paper as it was opened and refolded, and walked back to the bedside. Before she could ask Stella's answer, her eye rested on a letter in Ackerman's handwriting, lying open on the white covering. She started violently but managed to suppress an exclamation. Only that morning she had received herself a letter from the young

Northerner declaring his love in simple, honest fashion. She couldn't believe her eyes at first, but a second look convinced her of its reality. What puzzled her still more was to observe beside this letter a sheet of paper on which was drawn the diagram of the hall with the minute accuracy of an architect's plan, with Ackerman's notes interlining it.

"What shall I say?" she stammered in confusion.

Stella looked at her with a momentary start, smiled and answered:

"Tell Mr. Graham I have received and read his letter. I'll think it over this evening and reply to-morrow."

"Then I'll go," said Susie, taking her hand. "I'm so glad I saw you."

As she turned through the door her eye again was drawn irresistibly to Ackerman's letter. She returned to John Graham's office stunned by this puzzling discovery.

John was bitterly disappointed in the message she brought. Her long stay had raised in him the highest hope. His own surrender had been so complete and generous, that he could not conceive it possible that she would debate in cold blood for twenty-four hours the question of her answer. It seemed heartless and utterly cruel. He rebelled

in fierce futile protest.   He did not try to conceal
the bitterness of his disappointment from Susie,
and was too selfishly occupied with his own grief
to note the constraint in her manner as she hurried
home from his office, even before he had found
words in which to thank her for the delicate service
she had rendered him.

He sent for Alfred and got word to Aunt Julie
Ann that he wished to see her at her cottage after
supper.   He knew that Alfred had taken advantage of Isaac's long absence to renew his calls on
his former love.

When he arrived at nine o'clock Aunt Julie Ann
had placed a pot of coffee and a plate of tea-cakes
on a little table for him.

"What's de matter, honey?" she asked.

"I'm in great trouble, Aunt Julie Ann."

"Well, Mammy's baby knows who ter come
to when he's in trouble!" she said tenderly.   She
had always called him baby—this bronzed hero
of battle fields.   His thirty years meant nothing
to her except increasing faith in his manhood.
Since the day she first took his baby form in her
arms she had watched him grow in body and spirit
with a brooding mother pride.

"You must talk to Miss Stella for me," he
said.   "Get close to her Aunt Julie Ann, you're
a woman, and tell her all the good things you

remember about me. You know better than I do
—you understand? Make her smile again and
get her to see me."

"Now, you set down dar sir, an' drink dat
coffee an' tell me what you doin' gwine roun' here
mopin' an' pinin' yo' life out all 'about a gal don't
care two straws whedder you'se er livin' er dyin'.
I'd be shamed er myself, great big grown man lak
you is, what fit froo de war an' everybody say
gwine ter be de guvnor some day."

"Can't you get her to see me, Aunt Julie Ann?"
he interrupted, earnestly.

"Drink dat coffee, an' den I tell ye!"

"It's too hot for coffee—I'm not hungry—Tell
me now."

"Drink it fur Mammy, boy—I wants de grouns.
I'm gwine tell ye somefin when I looks in de
cup. I seed a vision las' night."

To humour her John drank the coffee in silence.

She took the empty cup, studied its message,
and looked into John's face.

"Yes, honey, hit's des lak I see hit las' night,
an' I warns ye! I see two purty gals—a fair one
and a dark one. Bof lubs ye—but dey's one er
slippin up behind yer back wid a shinin' knife in
her hand. Her long black hair is hangin' loose
on her white shoulders an' all twisted lak snakes.
I see her hide de knife in her bosom an' slip her

arms roun' yo neck. She kiss you an' blindfold ye wid her curly hair an' slip de knife from her bosom an' stab you froo de heart! Mammy's baby! Mammy's baby!"

The black woman's voice sank to a weird whisper full of tears and wild half-savage music as she seized John's hand.

"Don't come to de house no mo,' Marse John!" she pleaded.

"And why not?" he asked sharply.

"Case I look again in de vision an' I see her face plain—an' it wuz hers!"

"Whose?"

"Miss Stella, honey—I warns ye! she doan lub my baby—keep away from her!"

"Rubbish, Aunt Julie Ann; you've been having a nightmare."

"I see it all, des ez plain ez I sees you now—I warns ye!"

"I'll risk it," John laughed. "I'm hoping for good news to-morrow—please say your prayers for me to-night."

Yet in spite of his culture and the inheritance of centuries of knowledge, the voodoo message of his old nurse shrouded his spirit in deeper gloom. He walked home with a new sense of dread in his heart, wondering what answer she would send him to-morrow.

CHAPTER XII

THE TRAP IS SPRUNG

THE following morning when Stella, sitting up in bed, opened her mail and read Ackerman's report, the last doubt of John Graham's guilt was shattered.

"I have just learned," Ackerman wrote, "that a number of men of notoriously desperate character from the foot of the mountains were in Independence on the day before the tragedy and that a man by the name of Dan Wiley, their leader, reported in person to John Graham's office."

Stella sprang from her bed and began hurriedly to dress.

"Now God give me strength for the work I'm going to do!" she cried, with strangling rage. "To think that such a man should dare to speak to me of love—should dare to clasp my hand with the stain of my father's blood yet fresh on his! I could kill him with my own hand—coward, dastard, sneak, assassin! I hate him—I hate him!"

She threw herself on her bed again in a paroxysm of uncontrollable fury. She arose at length, calm, alert, her cheeks flushed with brilliant colour, her great eyes dilated wide and sparkling with courage.

The knocker struck sharply and she remembered with a start that Steve Hoyle had returned on the midnight train and would call this morning. She heard Maggie show Steve into the library.

Without waiting for her breakfast she hastened to meet him, and he plunged at once into the purpose of his call:

"Has John Graham yet confessed his leadership?"

"He will to-day," was the quiet answer.

"The fame of your desperate love affair has set the town agog," Steve laughed triumphantly.

"Doubtless," she replied moodily.

"I've everything arranged—the men are only waiting for the word."

"I prefer that the law take its course. I'm not ready to commit murder," she said emphatically.

"Nonsense! The law's a farce—Deliver him to his own men to be judged by the Klan which has set itself above the State. If he is the leader of the Invisible Empire he holds his own High Court. Let his men decide his fate. It's justice!"

Stella hesitated a moment and slowly said:

"When I learn from his own lips that he is the Chief of the Klan and find that there is no other way in which he can be made to pay the penalty of his crime, I'll deliver him to his men."

"They'll be ready to receive him."

"I shall know in twenty-four hours."

"I'll await your word," he answered eagerly, his eyes devouring her beauty.

Steve hurriedly left and Stella seated herself at her desk to write her answer to John Graham. Two attempts she tore up. The third suited her. In the centre of a sheet of paper she wrote two words:

"Come—Stella."

When John Graham received this note at eleven o'clock from the hands of her messenger, he felt before he broke the seal that it bore glad tidings.

He tore it open and with a cry of joy, tried to read, and the tears blinded him. He crushed the note in his hand and bowed his head on his desk, his whole being convulsed with emotion which he could not control. He rose at length, walked to his window, opened the note again and gazed at it until he broke into a joyous laugh, repeating the words:

"Come—Stella."

"The most wonderful letter I ever received," he exclaimed. "The longest, the richest, the deepest—the answering call of my mate! In all nature

there's no such cry. From out the shadows of
hell I lift my soul and answer, 'My love, I come!'"

In a moment he had forgotten every fear; and
all the pain, blind and hideous, of the last three
days was lost in a joy that lit the world with
splendour.

He called immediately on horseback and asked
her to ride with him through a beautiful wooded
road he had long wished to show her. Stella
caught the echo of his horse's hoofs with a shudder
as he approached the house. She had not heard
that sound on the gravelled roadway of the lawn
since the night she listened to the distant echoes
of the masqueraders as she stood beside the dead.

She accepted his suggestion and hastily des-
patched a message to Ackerman asking that he
await her return in her library at sundown as she
intended to spend the afternoon in the country on
important business.

At three o'clock they galloped out of Independence toward the river.

"My heart is too full now for speech," he said,
leaning toward her, his face radiant with happiness.

"I understand."

"Just to be near you is all I ask for a while.
It seems too good to be true. It has been a
century since I saw you."

She remained silent. The only visible response,

if any, was the quickening of her horse's pace at the unconscious touch of the little spur concealed beneath her skirts.

Her silence meant to him feelings too deep for words, and again his heart sang for joy.

Four miles out of town they left the main highway and turned into the narrow crooked road which wound along the banks of a creek through the densest forest in the county.

"I'm going to take you to 'Inwood,' General Gaston's place. The house was burned by Sherman's army, only the vine-covered ruins are standing now. It was the finest house ever built in the state, and many a gay party held high carnival there in the old days."

"I've heard my mother speak of it," she answered soberly, glancing at him from the corner of her eye. "In fact, it was there at a picnic one day that my father proposed to his sweetheart and my mother accepted him, and planned their elopement. How strange that you should have chosen to bring me to this place to-day!"

"You'll understand it later," he quickly responded.

"I hope you don't mean to kidnap me?"

"It might be advisable in view of the events of the past three days," he laughed.

She glanced about her at the deep shadows

of the great trees through which they had been passing for more than a mile and shot at him a sudden look of fear.

"Let's turn back," she said, flushing and reining her horse to a stand.

A look of pain clouded his face as he bent near.

"Surely, dearest, you can trust the man who worships you! Come, we are only a few hundred yards from the gate."

"Then I'll trust you that much further," she said with a light laugh, spurring her horse forward.

In a few minutes they passed through the ruined gate in the edge of the woods. The broken marble figures which once crowned the brick pillars lay beside the entrance among a mass of tangled blackberry briars. They had been pried from their places and hurled there by the bayonets of Sherman's men and had not been touched since.

The lawn, which once had spread its beautiful carpet of flowers and shrubbery in wide acres here in the heart of the ancient woods, had grown up in ugly broom straw and young pines, which were slowly strangling to death the more delicate forms of life. The dark fir trees, magnolia and holly, still flourished in luxury.

Towering in solemn, serried line on a gentle eminence still stood the six great white Corinthian pillars of the front façade of the house. Behind them in dark background a row of Norwegian firs, fifty years old, marked the sky line. The afternoon sun cast the shadows of the trees across the fluted marble of two of the pillars, while the other four shimmered in the splendour of the sunlight.

The capitals of the columns had fallen with the blazing ruins of the house, but the bases and tall beautiful fluted forms of each were yet perfect. The ivy which had grown on the sides of the stone steps had climbed in unbridled riot over one of them and hung in graceful festoons from the top.

To Stella's fancy they seemed grim white sentinels guarding the entrance to some vast empire of the dead.

"How still and death-like everything is," she said, with a timid glance about her. "We seem a thousand miles from life."

He took her hand.

"When I stand by your side, in every silent space I hear the beating of the wings of angels."

"The wings of the angel of Death here, I should think!" she said in strange subdued tones, as her eyelids drooped and she looked away.

"Away with such nonsense," he cried, cheerily. "I've something to do before I dare to speak to you again of the love that is in my heart."

He led her behind the towering columns, and, at the rear of the ruins of the heavy brick walls, entered the basement by a stairway half covered with fallen débris.

The floors of the first story which had been constructed of iron and cement foundations had remained unbroken. The basement, once entered below the ruins, was in a state of perfect preservation.

They entered the immense kitchen whose walls had once echoed with the voices of swarms of indolent well-fed slaves.

Stella looked about her in amazement, asking with a slight tremor in her voice:

"Why have you brought me here?"

"To place my life in your hands, joyously, without a single reservation," he said with deep earnestness. "You are in the council chamber of the Invisible Empire. Here its High Court of Life and Death was held."

Stella's breath quickened and she glanced at John with furtive eyes.

"I should have told you frankly at first. You had the right to know before you gave your life into my keeping."

He led her to the big wrought-iron range and opened one of its ovens, revealing the form of an old-fashioned safe.

Taking a huge key from his pocket, he opened the door and drew from it a package of papers.

"I am going to show you, my love, what no woman's eye ever saw before, the guarded secrets of the Invisible Empire, its signs, passwords, ritual and secret oath. In this act I now imperil no life save my own."

Stella's tapering fingers trembled as she turned the pages nervously and read its brief formulas.

"As Chief of the Klan I met here the leaders from each district."

"Then—you—are—the—Chief?" she slowly asked, bending low to hide her flushed face.

".Yes, I was the only Chief the Empire ever had in the state," he answered with a ring of boyish pride.

"And you bowed to no law save your own?" she asked in low tones.

"No."

"And you really did hold high courts of life and death?" she whispered.

"Yes, we were the sole guardians of white civilisation. It was a necessity—the last resort of desperation."

"You tried men here in secret, sentenced them without a hearing, executed them at night without warning, mercy or appeal?"

"It had to be—there was no other way. A

million soldiers girded us with their bayonets. We had to strike under a mantle of darkness and terror, where the power of resistance was weakest, the blow unsuspected and discovery impossible."

"How terrible!" she interrupted with a shudder. "And yet," she went on with a sudden flash of her eye, "its mystery and its daring fascinate me! Would you do something just to please a romantic fancy of mine?"

"I have but one desire in life—to please your fancy," he cried.

"Come here with me again, day after to-morrow night, and dress in your costume as Chief of the High Court of the Klan. Bring some lanterns and we'll light it up—it's just a fancy of mine—will you do it?"

"You're not afraid to be here alone with me at night?"

"Why should I? I love to do daring unconventional things. Besides, do we not belong to each other now?"

"You do love me?" he whispered.

"Do you doubt it?"

"Kiss me!" he pleaded, bending closer.

With a sudden shudder she drew away.

"Not yet! you must be patient. I've a lot of silly notions. That's one of them. I'll learn, no doubt."

"I'll try to teach you," he laughed—"and be content to touch your hand until my desire shall be yours."

They rode swiftly home, John's soul in a warm glow of happiness. Stella spoke scarcely a word, but her cheeks were flushed and about her deep brown eyes a curious smile was constantly playing.

He left her at the door and as he pressed her hand softly said:

"You scarcely spoke the whole way home— tell me what were you thinking about?"

"I don't know—perhaps dreaming of your terrible court—of a man being condemned to death without knowing it!"

"Yet a smile was playing about your beautiful face?"

Stella suddenly burst into half hysterical laughter:

"Of course, how can you doubt that I was happy! I'll tell you all my thoughts to-morrow night."

"Shall we go on horseback?"

"Yes, but I wish to go alone; I'll meet you there at dusk," she replied with another strange laugh, waving her hand as he mounted his horse and galloped away.

She closed the door and with quick nervous step, crossed the hall and passed into the library, confronting Ackerman.

"John Graham is the Chief of the Ku Klux Klan—he has confessed to me!" she whispered excitedly. "I have arranged everything for his arrest day after to-morrow evening at their secret meeting place."

"Then our work is complete," he said with a ring of triumph.

"And his execution is a certainty?"

"I haven't the remotest idea that Graham himself can ever be convicted of the murder of Judge Butler—but your discovery is of tremendous importance."

"He—cannot—be—convicted!" Stella gasped.

"No, but the Invisible Empire will be in ruins in forty-eight hours," he replied, seizing his hat. "Excuse me now, I have work of the gravest importance to-night. Thanks for the promptness with which you have kept your promise."

Before Stella could speak he was gone. With a scowl on her beautiful brow, she called Maggie:

"Tell Mr. Steve Hoyle I wish to see him here immediately."

CHAPTER XIII

FOR LOVE'S SAKE

STEVE'S response to Stella's call was prompt. He entered the library with heavy, firm step, a flush of triumph on his sleek handsome animal face.

"He has betrayed the Klan to you?" he asked with eagerness.

"Sit down," she responded coolly, an accent of resentment rising in her voice. Before I answer that important question, I've something I wish to ask you."

"Anything you like," he answered suavely.

"And I want the truth," she continued, with increasing emphasis.

"I'll give it to you if it's in my power."

"You haven't done it always," was the firm retort.

"You wish to know about the men on whom I rely to execute justice on John Graham?"

"Yes, who are they?"

"Members of the Klan from the hills—innocent men on whom he wreaked his vengeance in the most brutal and inhuman manner without a trial."

"You are sure they are members of the Klan?"

"Certainly."

"They will come to arrest and try him, dressed in the same costumes the men wore the night my father was killed?"

"Yes."

"Have you hired these men to assassinate him?" she suddenly asked, piercing Steve with her great eyes.

"My God, no!" he protested.

"What will they do?"

"Why, try him by his own laws, of course," Steve answered vaguely.

"What laws?"

"The law of the Order which forbids an officer to abuse his power by using it for personal ends as he did in the murder of the Judge."

"Why have they not tried him before?"

"The feeling against him was not strong enough."

"And now?"

"If he has betrayed the Klan, by his own laws he can be torn limb from limb, so long as a shred of its power remains."

"He could not be put to death for telling the secrets of the Klan to the woman he loves?"

"Yes."

"And he knows this?"

"Of course."

"A big, glorious, beautiful thing, a love like that, isn't it?" she cried with strange elation, tears flashing from her eyes.

"From the woman's point of view, perhaps it is—from that of the man whose life he puts in peril, hardly."

"But from the woman's point of view! yes— and judged by her standard, cowards who hedge and lie and fear to do such things don't measure very high beside him—do they? I'm afraid, Steve, your love is a weak thing. It would be a pity to kill a man who would dare death to please the fancy of the woman he loves—now, wouldn't it?"

"Such a man, for example, as he who sneaked under cover of the night and struck your father dead at your feet without a chance to defend himself," Steve sneered.

"Yes! That's the hideous thought that strangles me!" she cried, her breast heaving with a tumult of emotion, her breath coming in gasps of passion.

"You are going to falter and give up?" he asked indignantly.

Stella ignored his question and said in even tones as though talking to herself:

"I had intended to have the United States

marshals arrest him dressed in the Klan costume at their meeting place."

"And now?" Steve broke in eagerly.

"I don't know what to do. I'll be frank with you, Steve—I never expected to keep my promise to marry you—I never really expected to face such a choice. There are times when I like you. There's evil in me, as there is in you—cruelty, pride, selfishness—I feel our kinship. But I don't love you, and the closer I get to you the less I love you."

"You'll learn to love me—I'll wait," he broke in.

"The reason why I like you less and less," she went on, "is that I feel other forces in me which are not evil—big, generous impulses, and aspirations for things beautiful and true and good that you have never felt and could never understand."

"Which some other man might develop," he snapped. "Well, play the baby act then, and give it all up."

"No, I've made up my mind to have the life of the man who took my father's. It's the one supreme passion which dominates my soul and body."

"He has confessed to you then?" Steve cried breathlessly.

"Yes."

"Where will the men meet you?"

"At Inwood immediately after dark, day after to-morrow," she answered firmly.

"It's too early.   Nine o'clock is better.   The men will have time for careful preparation."

"I'll be with him in the basement.   He will be in the Klan costume; I wish him arrested and tried in that."

"It shall be exactly as you wish," said Steve, his eyes sparkling with triumph.   "And your signal to the men?"

"Will be a light in the window of the basement."

"I understand—Inwood—nine o'clock at night, day after to-morrow."

Stella's answer was scarcely a whisper:

"Yes."

CHAPTER XIV

THE JUDGMENT HALL OF FATE

STELLA made excuses to John Graham for not being able to see him before their appointment to meet at Inwood, and on the afternoon of the day fixed rode out of town at four o'clock alone.

Her unconventional ways had ceased to excite comment in Independence since her extraordinary conduct in refusing to wear mourning for her father. There could be no graver breach of the traditions of good society than this in the eyes of her neighbours, and so long as she remained within the pale of respectability any other feat she might perform would be of minor interest.

She rode rapidly, her mind in a tumult of excitement over the daring act of revenge she meant to wreak to-night on the man who had wronged her beyond the power of human forgiveness. Single-handed and alone she had mastered his will and brought him to her feet. Single-handed and alone she had decided the question of his life and death. And this afternoon she wished to ride alone to the place appointed for his judgment.

In spite of her resolution to mete out the sternest justice to John Graham, the memory of his passionate words of love, the deep tenderness with which he had hovered about her, and the utter trust he had shown during their last meeting, began to torment her.

Had they met under fair conditions she could have loved him. She began to see it clearly now. His sincerity, his fiery emotions, his romantic extravagances, the old-fashioned chivalry with which he worshipped her were very sweet. The complete and generous surrender he had made, placing his life absolutely in her hands, began to glow with poetry in her imagination.

He had always possessed the faculty of drawing out the best that was in her. Somehow she had never been able to hate him as she ought in his presence. There was something contagious in the spirit of love with which his whole personality seemed to radiate. She had begun to feel at home with him as with no other man she had ever met.

"Oh, dear, I'm sorry!" she sighed, as she entered the deep woods. Unconsciously she reined her horse to a stand, and was startled from her reverie by a tear rolling down her cheek and falling on her glove. "What a fool I am!" she cried in anger. "I'd better turn back now. I'm a chicken-hearted coward when put to the test. I'm scared out of

my senses at the size of the task I've undertaken—
that's what's the matter—I, who have boasted of
my strength and shouted my triumph over a strong
man's conquest."

Another tear rolled down her cheek. She
brushed it away with an angry stroke.

"Suppose I find too late that I'm in love with
him!" she exclaimed, helplessly.

Her horse moved on without her urging or
recognising it, so absorbed had she become in the
battle raging within her heart.

"What is love?" she mused aloud. "I wonder
how it feels to really love?—Love him?—nonsense
—I hate the very ground he walks on—the self-
centred, proud, bigoted, narrow-minded fan-
atic! I've sworn to avenge my father's death. I'll
do it. Let him come to-night to the judgment
hall of his own making. I'll prove myself a woman,
and do my country a service when I hand him over
to justice."

She touched her horse with the whip, and he
bounded forward in a swift gallop, and in a few
minutes she passed into the old lawn and saw the
flash of the white ghost-like columns among the
dark firs.

Again she found herself recalling the silly
extravagances of his talk as they entered the
grounds two days before.

"What was it he said about angels?" she mused
with a smile. "Yes, I remember. Somehow I
seem to remember them all!—'When I stand by
your side, in every silent space I hear the beating
of the wings of angels'—and I liked it! what a
fool a woman is! and tried to convince myself
that I didn't like it by adding, 'the wings of the
angel of death,' only because I felt my hate grow
weak under a silly compliment—well, I'm done
with his maudlin love-making. It's judgment
day."

She dismounted, tied her horse, and wandered
down the little crooked pathway to the famous
spring at the foot of the hill where many a lover had
lingered in days long past and poured out the old
story that remains eternal in its youth. She
wondered at the mad resolution of her mother,
taken perhaps on this very spot twenty-five years
ago, that had led her to break the bonds of blood,
throw to the winds every tie of tenderness that
bound her to the earth, and brave the scorn of her
own proud world, all for the sake of the son of a
poor white man—because she loved him!

Why did people do such idiotic things? Why
should a woman thus sink her soul and body in
the fortunes of a man? She couldn't understand it.

"Surely this is the miracle of miracles of human
life!" she murmured. "I wonder if John Graham

was crazy when he said that night on the lawn:
'If you should send me from your presence now,
I'd laugh at Death, for I have tasted Life!' Why
do I keep thinking of what he has said?—Perhaps
because he may die to-night!"

She sprang to her feet, clasped her hands nervously and began to cry—softly at first, and then
with utter abandonment, sinking again to the
ground and burying her face in her arm.

"Oh, dear! oh, dear! I'm lonely and heartsick
and afraid!" she sobbed. I wish I had a friend
to share my secret, advise and help me—yes, such
a friend as he would be!—he'd know what I ought
to do—and I know what he'd say, too—that I'm
proud and cruel and selfish—that I'm doing a
hideous, unnatural thing—well I'm not! the
impulse for vengeance is God's first law—I know it
because I feel it, deep, instinctive, resistless!—and
I'm going to do it! I'm going to do it!—I hate him!
I hate him!"

She rose and returned to the ruins, and sat down
on the steps between the white columns. The sun
was sinking through an ocean of filmy clouds,
reflecting in rapid changes every colour ever
dreamed in the soul of the artist. She watched
in deep breathless reverence, until the sense of
loneliness again overpowered her and she sprang
up with restless energy exclaiming:

"I meant to explore that room before he comes—I must do it."

She descended the steps and stopped before the dark entrance. It hadn't seemed so dark the other day with him. It was earlier in the day of course. Why had she paused? The question angered her. She was afraid to go through the long dark corridor alone—that was the disgusting truth.

She turned back to await his coming. What a foolish contradiction. She would wait for the protection of the wretch she meant to deliver to-night to—death!

She returned with quick angry strides to the columns, and leaned against one of their friendly sides. In the gathering twilight they seemed human and sheltering in their protection. She wished he would come. A dozen times she looked toward the gate and thought she heard the beat of his horse's hoof in the distance.

Dusk settled into darkness and still he did not come. The moon rose and touched the tall pillars above with a magic glow of mellow light, and a whip-poor-will struck the first note of his thrilling song beneath the bush at her feet.

With a shudder, she moved to the outer column and waited with increasing impatience and alarm. The wildest fears began to fill her fancy. Why had she dared this mad task alone? For some unaccountable reason she had not reckoned on being alone.

Was it possible that she had been so illogical, so utterly bereft of reason that the idea of his companionship had filled her imagination? Surely she had not been such a fool! She knew Steve Hoyle would accompany those men, beyond a doubt, and join her after the affair was over, but she had not given Steve a thought. He had been but a cog in the wheel of things that had swiftly moved to the tragic crisis which she now faced for the first time. She looked at her watch in the bright moonlight and it was half past eight. What if he failed to come! Would she be glad or angry? The tumult of feeling had reached a point of intensity that paralysed her powers of reasoning— she didn't know. A single sense remained, the consciousness of chilling loneliness.

With a throb of joy she caught at last the quick hoof-beat of John's horse sweeping through the gateway in a furious gallop.

He leaped to the ground, and hurried to her side.

"I'm awfully sorry!" he cried, seizing both her hands with eager tenderness. "A most unexpected thing occurred which delayed me thirty minutes. I'll explain to you later. Come, I'm hungry to see your dear face in the light of these

lanterns in that gloomy old room below. I've
a thousand things to tell you. Life will be too
short a time in which to tell it all. I hope you've
been very lonely and hungry for me to come ?"

"I must confess, my heart began to fail me once
or twice," she said seriously, while he felt her hand
trembling.

He stooped to light a lantern, and she caught his
arm.

"Wait, not yet—the moon is shining brightly—
we don't need it."

"But you'll stumble on those dark stairs in the
corridor."

"No matter, wait," she urged nervously; "I'll
hold your arm—you know the way."

"Yes, I know the way," he laughed. "Come
then, your slightest whim is law."

He drew her little hand through his arm and
picking his steps carefully, led her down through
the tangled débris and along the dark corridor
without once stumbling, the timid figure clinging
close to his side.

"You see a revolutionist soon learns to find his
way in the dark without a light," he said, as they
emerged into the kitchen whose wide space was
lighted by the moonbeams streaming through the
windows.

He released her arm, placed the lantern and a

bundle he carried on the top of the range, and said with a laugh:

"Now, shall the actor make up for his part? I've the costume all ready. This is the palace of the queen to-night. I have been commanded to appear before her!"

She gave no answer.

He bent and kissed her hand and found it cold and trembling violently.

"You feel the chill of this old basement," he said with tender solicitude. "I'll light the lantern at once."

She caught his hand.

"No! No!—I—prefer it like this—the moonlight is enough."

"All right," he answered gaily. "Shall I don my robes as ruler of the Invisible Empire to please the fancy of Your Majesty?"

He opened the bundle and shook out the long white ulster-like disguise with its double cross of scarlet and gold.

"Put it back—I'm not ready yet!" she gasped.

"You'll laugh and chat a while with the audience before the curtain goes up on the drama!—good! I've a lot to say. Sit here in the window while I tell you something."

He led her to the low casement of the window and seated her by his side.

She sprang to her feet instantly, grasping at her heart, her breath coming in quick gasps:

"What's that!—Listen!"

He took her hand soothingly:

"Why, it's only our horses neighing to each other."

"You're sure?" she whispered.

"Of course."

"I thought it was something else," she faltered.

"My poor little darling! This has been too much for your nerves—you should have allowed me to come with you."

"Yes, I'm afraid I did make a mistake!" she said in low strained tones.

"Well, there's nothing to be afraid of now—is there?" he said assuringly.

"No! there's nothing to be afraid of now—is there?" she laughed hysterically, and suddenly stopped with a suppressed scream.

"My darling!" he exclaimed.

"Listen! Listen! My God, what's that?"

"It's nothing dear."

"It is! Listen! I hear them coming!"

"Impossible, my child, we're all here!" he laughed. "How could you guess there was anyone coming except you and me?"

"Oh, dear, you don't understand, and I can't explain!" she went on frantically. She looked at her watch and couldn't see.

"Quick, strike a match and see what time it is—we can get away!" she whispered.

He struck the match and saw her eyes gleaming with a strange madness. Stella blew the match out, seized his arm and drew him from the window.

"Not there—by the window—over here in this corner."

"He struck another match and she masked its light from the window, staring with wide-set eyes at the hands of her watch.

"It's half past nine. It's too late!" she said hopelessly.

"Come, come, my darling, remember that I am by your side—nothing can harm you except the tongue of gossip, and you've shown your contempt for that. Sit down here again in the moonlight and let me tell you the story of my love."

He led her back to the window and she sank tremblingly by his side.

"I've never had the chance to tell you," he began, with low passionate tenderness, "what a wonderful thing your love has been in my life. The night I met you, I went to your house drunk, with murder in my heart, determined to use the lawless power I wielded to crush your father. I was about to leave with a threat to kill him on my lips. It was no idle threat then. I had entered the vault, pushed open its massive door, stepped inside and saw the way was open."

"The night you came first, you entered alone the secret way?" she interrupted.

"Yes, I meant to use it if necessary."

"But you never did! You never did!" she whispered.

"How could I, dearest! I saw your face that night for the first time, heard the low music of your voice, touched your hand, and I was a new man! Love, not hate, has ruled me since. I disbanded the Klan immediately and ordered my men never again to use its power."

"Disbanded the Klan!" she repeated with choking surprise.

"Yes, and a dastard reorganised it as a local order to further his low ambitions. I've done my best to hold in check their crimes and follies. I warned your father of danger the night those fools came. In a madness of love, fear and jealous rage I came down to the house, sat there in dumb pain and watched your beautiful form whirl past the lighted window until I could endure it no longer."

Stella strangled a sob.

"I've reproached myself a hundred times I didn't prevent that masquerade by force. I might have done it. I had some faithful old soldiers from the foothills in town that day whom I had used to capture the scoundrels who committed the outrage on old Nicaroshinski."

"Hush! hush! before I scream!" Stella cried in anguish, placing her hand on his lips.

Suddenly a white figure stood before the window and his whistle rang through the still night.

Stella sprang to her feet gasping, with horror:

"My God! they've come: I must save you! Hide! Hide and give me your revolver—they shall not take you—quick—quick—hide!"

"But, my dear, there's not the slightest danger. No man who wears that uniform will lift his hand against me—see, I'm going to answer his call with my own signal."

He lifted the whistle to his lips and she snatched it from his grasp.

"Don't! Don't for God's sake, don't! you don't understand—Oh!—John—darling—I love you! I love you!"

She threw herself into his arms and kissed him, passionately sobbing.

"I've tried to hate you, dear, but I couldn't—I couldn't—I know now I've loved you always! I must save you, God help me!"

"Well, sir?" called a voice without.

"It's all right! Come in, boys!" he answered before Stella could stop him. She huddled in his arms paralysed for the moment with terror,

"You must not!—they will kill you, dear!" she moaned in agony.

"Nonsense, child, the boys have only a little surprise for us."

Their feet were already echoing in the corridor and their voices could be heard in whispers and low laughter.

"Hide! please, for the love of God!" she gasped. With sudden fierce strength she pressed him into the shadows and stood panting before him, while the silent ghost-like figures ranged themselves solemnly around the room.

"Stella, my dear, you must not suffer like this—there is no danger, these are all my men."

"Your men!—your men!" she cried, bewildered.

"Yes, I brought them here to-night in full costume to make a little play complete for the fancy of a queen!"

"My darling," she sobbed, sinking in his arms.

"We unexpectedly met some ugly customers from the hills we had seen once before. A little pitched battle delayed us thirty minutes, but none of our boys were hurt."

"Kiss me!" she whispered.

A distant whistle rang through the woods and the picket outside answered.

"What's that?" Stella gasped.

"He blew the signal, 'message for the Chief';

he's from town, I'm afraid," John answered slowly.

A horse's hoof echoed on the flagstones before the columns, and in a moment the picket rushed to the window.

"Bad news, sir!"

"What is it?" John asked quietly:

"A regiment of United States cavalry slipped into town just after dark."

"I've been looking for it," John broke in. "Well?"

"A squadron has surrounded Mrs. Wilson's boarding house to wait for you."

"Merciful God! what have I done!" Stella sobbed inaudibly.

John touched her hand soothingly at the sound of her sob, bent low and whispered tenderly:

"It's all right—dearest—you love me!"

Book III—Prisoner and Traitor

CHAPTER I

THE ARREST

THE news of the arrival of the regiment of cavalry, and the swift silent way in which they had struck their first blow, brought to John Graham at once a sharp realisation of the danger of his men.

Releasing Stella, he turned to the white figures gathered in an excited group and in short sharp accents said:

"I thank you boys for your kindness in coming to the little masquerade we had prepared to celebrate the announcement of my engagement to the woman who is the queen of my heart. Sorry the Yanks have interrupted us. Get home as fast as your horses can carry you. Burn your costumes the minute you reach a safe place. Hide them under your saddles as usual until you can burn them. Leave one at a time and go home by unused roads if possible. And listen—every man of you who can, should leave the state in twenty-four hours and stay until the trouble blows over."

"What are you goin' to do?" asked a tall masked figure.

"Don't worry, Dan. I'll look out for myself. You boys do the same and do it quick."

"We'll stan' by you if ye give the word," persisted Dan.

John left Stella's side, stepped to the men and growled:

"I've given the word. Run, and run like hell!"

"We don't like the orders, Chief, but orders is orders—git boys!"

The men quickly disappeared, and John took Stella's hand:

"Come, dearest, we must go."

"Yes," she answered, timidly clinging to his arm and holding him back.

"We must hurry," he urged.

"I won't hurry," she said with tender wilfulness.

"When a woman won't, she won't," John laughed.

She gently stroked his hand and slowly slipped her arm in his as she allowed him to lead her out into the moonlight beside the white silent pillars.

"Wait here until I bring the horses," John said, gently disengaging his arm.

Stella clung to him firmly.

"No, don't go yet. Why hurry? Let them

wait. I wish to be alone with you for a while here
on this beautiful spot. It's all so new and
wonderful. This knowing that I love and am
loved! I've just begun to live the past hour. I'm
afraid to go back to the world."

"I must face some stern realities to-night. But
you love me. That's the only thing of any importance. What do jails matter? They can only
imprison the body—my soul will follow you,
hover about you, laugh and cry with you day and
night, waking or dreaming."

"They won't put you in jail to-night, dear?"
she asked, piteously.

"Yes."

"Then you shall not give yourself up to them!
You'll let me have my own way now that you
know that I love you, won't you, John dear?
There! I've called your name for the first time—
haven't I?—I love your name!—You're not going
to give up to them—are you?"

"I see no other way, dearest."

"You told your men to fly. Our horses are
fresh. We can put miles between us and these
troops before day. I'll go with you, just as I am
in this riding habit—no matter—I'll get a dress
somewhere when you're out of danger."

He slipped his arm about her, bent his tall form,
and stopped her with a kiss.

"How sweet to hear you talk this beautiful nonsense!"

"I mean it," she hurried on earnestly. "We must leave to-night, I don't know what they may do to you. Something terrible—maybe—I can't think of it! Something may happen to separate us. I want to feel your hand clasping mine like this forever!"

He answered by crushing the little hand in his.

"You won't go back and let them arrest you, will you, John?" she pleaded, a sob catching her voice.

He was silent and a smile played about his mouth.

"Answer me, John dear! You must do as I say because life is too sweet and beautiful to lose it! You will leave if I go with you—won't you? My whim you said should be your law. This is my whim, my heart's desire. Get the horses now, and we'll make them fly as far from Independence to-night as their heels can carry us! You'll do this because I ask it—won't you, darling?"

The little head began to droop, the voice broke, and she lay sobbing in his arms.

He held her close for a moment.

"You know this is impossible, dear!"—he said tenderly.

"Yes, I know!" she sobbed.

"My business is to save others now."

"At least, you'll go by the house and stay with me a little while?"

"They'll think I'm hiding."

"Who cares what they think? I can't go home alone, can I?"

"Of course, I'll stop a moment. And now we must hurry."

He brought the horses and they galloped back to town in silence. Along a dark rough place of the road, they slowed down to a walk, and his hand sought hers.

"What a strange ending to the most wonderful day of my life!" she suddenly cried with passionate tenderness.

"Why strange?" he asked. "I never had a doubt that you would love me. It was written in the Book of Life."

"But I didn't know it until to-night."

"Tell me, dear," he pleaded; "what sudden flash revealed the truth?"

"Don't ask me!" she said with a shiver. "I'll tell you some day."

"Why not now? This has been a wonderful day for me. I shall never live its like again. I heard for the first time the one woman I love, the only woman I ever loved, the one woman I shall love forever, speak the sweetest words that ever fell from human lips."

"I love you—I love you!" she softly repeated.

"But tell me how you came to know it to-day?" he urged.

"It's a secret—one I fear that will give me many an hour of anguish. I'll tell you, dear—but not now."

"I'll share it with you when you'll let me."

"Not this one, John. I need to bear it alone to keep me humble, and sweeten with suffering and fear the bitter, selfish impulses that fight within me. Oh, I want to be good and tender and beautiful and true now!"

"How full of strange moods you've been to-night!" he exclaimed.

"Have I dear?"

She caught his hand and pressed it tenderly.

The lights of the town flashed in view from the hill.

They galloped boldly down the main street and into the lawn. As they passed the cabin at the gate, Isaac's face appeared a moment at the door.

"I didn't know old Isaac had returned?" John remarked.

"Nor did I," she replied; "he must have come with those troops."

A tremor caught her voice as she recalled that Ackerman was in communication with Isaac, and

the cords she had been winding about the man by
her side began slowly to tighten around her own
throat.

He tried to leave her at the door, but she drew
him inside.

"You can't go yet."

"I must hurry, my love," he protested. "Those
men will think I'm a coward. I should have been
at home when they called."

"Sh!"——

She placed her hand over his lips, ignoring his
plea.

"I've a little experiment to make. My whim is
law. Go stand there in the alcove with your hat
in your hand fumbling it."

Laughing with girlish excitement she pressed
him into the exact spot he stood the night she first
met him, drew back, and gazed tenderly into his
face, her big brown eyes dancing with the hysterical
strain of the deep half-conscious fear for his safety
which had begun to strangle her.

"Have you forgotten the first scene in the drama
of our life?" she asked, slowly approaching him
with extended hand.

He clasped it with a smile.

"I shall not forget it if I live to be a hundred
years old," he said reverently.

"And yet, you are trying to hurry away from me

to-night again.   Don't you like the picture as well now?"

"A thousand times better, dearest," he cried. "The love that shines in your eyes will make radiant the darkest hour of life. I've nothing now to fear. Perfect love has cast out fear. My way's a shining one whether it leads to a palace or a prison."

"Come into the dining room," she whispered, leading him through the door and seating herself at the head of the table. "You remember the night we sat together here?"

"Do I!"

"Would you believe me if I told you that I tried to make you love me that night?"

"You said you tried to hate me."

"But we can't always do what we try—can we?" she asked wistfully.

"You did that night I'm sure."

"And yet, I'm failing to-night!" she sobbed, unable to keep back the tears, "just when I've told you that I love you, and the joy and wonder of it all has begun to light the world. Before I've thought only of myself. To-night I'm thinking only of you, my sweetheart! Just as I've learned to speak your name I feel you slipping away from me—oh, John darling, what will they do to you? Tell me—tell me!"

"They can only put me in jail to-night."

"But they shall not—they shall not!" she moaned, clinging close to him. "You shall not let them! You shall not leave this house except to fly with me."

Stella's words choked into sudden silence at the shrill angry notes of Aunt Julie Ann's voice ringing in the hall:

"Git out er dis house, I tells ye, 'fo I bus' yo head open wid dis door weight."

"Mind your own business," snapped the angry reply.

"I'se mindin' my own business. Git out dat door, an' knock 'fo yer come in! An' I lets yer in when I gits ready—when my mistis say yer kin come!"

"Faith, an' I'll slap ye head off ye shoulders, if ye don't kape still," growled the trooper.

"What do you want in here, yer low-life slue-footed Yankee?"

"If it's just the same ter ye, I wants Mr. John Graham, me dusky maiden!"

John suddenly released himself from Stella's clinging form and stepped through the door into the hall.

"I'm John Graham. What is it?"

"You're my prisoner, sir, ye'll have to come with me!"

"I'm ready."

The sergeant took a step toward John, drawing a pair of handcuffs from his pocket.

Stella sprang between them, her eyes blazing with rage:

"How dare you enter my house without my permission?"

The sergeant stopped in sheer amazement at the fury of her outburst. Recovering himself with a smile he replied:

"Axin yer pardon m'am, it may be rude, but hit ain't writ in our book of etiquette ter knock at the front door when we're huntin' fer a man charged with murder."

"But he's not guilty!" Stella stormed.

"I believe ye, Miss—ye'd have an easy time with me. But I ain't the Coort!"

"Stella, dear," John pleaded.

"Leave this house!" Stella cried with fury.

"Sure m'am, but yer friend comes wid me," said the sergeant, taking another step toward John.

"I tell you he's not guilty! It's all a mistake. I'll explain to your commander in the morning."

John smiled in spite of himself.

"Stella dear, this is nonsense. The sergeant is acting under orders. I must go at once."

"Ye see, m'am!" said the sergeant with a polite bow.

"All right then, sergeant," said Stella, suddenly changing her tone, "I'll excuse you for your rudeness; I'll go with you."

"You mustn't, my love," John protested.

"Yes, I'm going with you, but I've had nothing to eat. We must have supper—it's waiting. Aunt Julie Ann, show the sergeant downstairs and give him supper. Mr. Graham will be ready in half an hour, sergeant."

The trooper looked doubtfully at John and at Stella, smiling.

"All right m'am. It's agin my principles as a soldier to leave a good supper to spoil—an', axin yer pardon agin, I'll station one o' me men at each door an' window to make sure we wont lose any of our party durin' the festivities. It'll be more sociable like to feel that we're all here."

The sergeant placed his men and followed Aunt Julie Ann to the kitchen.

Stella drew John to the old davenport:

"Quick, John darling, through the old secret way—the way of love——"

"Dearest!" he said reproachfully.

She extended her hand to press the spring in the panel.

"Quick, the soldier at the door can't see you. I'll stand in front. Wait for me in the vault. I'll let them search the house and when they go, I'll join you and we can leave before daylight."

"I must face it. There's no other way."

"Yes, yes, this way—the old sweet way of love! I can't let them take you—you're mine now—I love you—I love you!—John, dear, he has big ugly handcuffs. He was going to put them on you—didn't you see him?"—her voice faltered.

"Yes, I saw him."

"I can't stand it, John, I can't—oh, dear, you don't understand, and I can't explain—You love me?"

"Better than life and deeper than death."

"And yet you refuse my heart's desire?"

"Only in this. I'm done with lawlessness. I'm not a coward. I've led a successful revolution. It had to be, and now with silent lips I'll face my accusers."

A hot tear fell on his hand.

"Come, dearest, you must help me," he pleaded.

"Yes, yes, I will," she faltered, brushing the tears away. "Come then, we will have this one little supper together, shall we not?"

"Yes. I want to look across that old table into your face again."

He chatted gaily through the supper and she sat silent, choking back the sobs, unable to eat.

The sergeant bowed at the door:

"Axin yer pardon m'am, but I must hurry now."

John rose and the trooper again drew his handcuffs, Stella watching him with wide-set eyes.

"I'm sorry, sir, I'll have to put 'em on."

"It's all right, sergeant," he answered.

Stella sprang between them and placed a trembling little hand on the trooper's.

"Please, sergeant!"

"Orders, m'am, I'm sorry."

"Please—for—my—sake—don't. He'll go with you. I tried to get him to fly with me, and he wouldn't. You won't put them on him—will you? For my sake?"

Her voice sank to the softest music of tears. The sergeant hesitated a moment and said gruffly:

"All right, for your sake, m'am, I won't."

John stooped and kissed her. The door closed behind him and with a low piteous moan Stella sank to the floor, crying:

"God have mercy on me!"

CHAPTER II

THROUGH PRISON BARS

AN IMMENSE crowd had gathered at the hotel awaiting John's arrival. The news of his arrest had stirred the town to feverish excitement.

Without turning to the right or left, or answering a look of recognition, he marched between two soldiers through the mass of men and boys in the office and climbed the stairs to the rooms of the United States Commissioner who was waiting to receive him.

The Commissioner handed him the warrant and he merely glanced at its title:

"THE UNITED STATES *versus* JOHN GRAHAM
CONSPIRACY AND MURDER"

"I shall hold you without bail, Mr. Graham," said the Commissioner.

John merely nodded his head.

"To the county jail, sergeant!"

The soldiers turned and John descended the stairs, and again passed through the crowd, his head erect, his face an immovable mask.

In fifteen minutes the heavy bolt shot into place
and he was a prisoner awaiting trial for life, locked
in a filthy cell of the common jail of the county
of Independence.

He had often been to this jail as a lawyer to
interview prisoners whom he had defended at
various times, but he had paid no attention to the
building. The complaints of the discomforts of
the jail he had always taken as a humorous
contribution to life.

He was amazed to discover that the place into
which he had been suddenly thrust was an inner
room opening into a corridor with no means of
light or ventilation save the single iron-grilled door
—a veritable hell-hole whose heat was so stifling
and air so foul with disgusting odours he could
scarcely breathe. By the rays of the little kerosene
lamp which hung in the corridor, flickering,
sputtering and stinking, he saw that there was not
a trace of furniture in the room, not even a pile of
straw on which to sleep. The floor had evidently
not been swept in a year, the dust lay in piles, and
the room had just been vacated by four perspiring
Negro convicts who had been removed to the
penitentiary to serve sentences for burglary, arson
and murder.

It was impossible to sit down, it was unthinkable to lie down, and so for five hours back and

forth he walked the length of his cell like a caged panther.

For the first hour his proud spirit was sustained by the enormity of the degradation thus heaped upon him. He felt sure that such treatment was given him for a purpose. He knew that all the prisoners of the county were not treated as swine. In his anger he paused once, determined to demand a chair or bed of some kind, and found that he could only make his wants known by yelling down two flights of stairs to the guard who stood at the outer door of the last floor. He could not thus humiliate himself.

For the first time he realised what it meant to be deprived not only of the comforts but the common decencies of human life. In fierce anger he silently raved for two hours and then a strange calm came over his soul. His hands grasped the iron bars of the door and he stood as if in a trance while the unconscious minutes lengthened into hours. A beautiful face bent above him. Her voice, low and tender with the music of love, filled all space. The stifling cell vanished. He was in the open fields with her hand in his. He woke with a laugh, and caught the glint of the first beams of the rising sun stealing through the window of the corridor.

"A beautiful face bent above him"

A Negro boy brought his breakfast of corn bread and bacon in a dirty tin plate.

John looked at it a minute with a curious smile:

"No, thank you, my boy, I've just had my breakfast of ambrosia. I'll take a chair, however, if the jailor can spare one!"

"Yassah, I'll tell 'im when I goes down," he replied. "But I spec dey ain't none lef. We got lots er boarders now."

He placed the plate on the floor by the door, and grinned.

"Dey wuz er young lady come ter see ye las' night, sah, but dey wouldn't let 'er in!"

John smiled.

"What time was it?"

"Bout two er clock."

"Yes, I saw her," John slowly said with a strange look in his deep-set eyes. "She came up and stayed with me until sunrise."

The Negro backed cautiously away muttering.

"He got 'em sho!" and darted down the steps.

The fact that he was being kept in solitary confinement and refused communication of any kind with friend or counsel, roused every force of John Graham's character.

When the Attorney General who had come down from Washington called at ten o'clock he greeted him with a laugh through the bars of his door:

"Excuse my lack of hospitality, General Champion," he said; "I'd offer you a chair, but the hotel is crowded and we're short of chairs just now."

"Haven't you a chair or a bed in your cell?" he enquired, peering in. "It's an outrage. Bring two chairs here at once!" he thundered to the attendant.

"Mr. Graham," said the General cordially, "I've hastened to you as a friend. I was a member of Congress with your uncle. We were warm personal friends. I've known several of your people, and always found them the salt of the earth."

"Thanks," John interrupted, a smile playing about the corners of his eyes.

"I wish to be of help to you if you will let me. It has long been known to the Department of Justice that you are the Chief of the Klan in North Carolina."

"I congratulate the Department of Justice on the attainment of such interesting knowledge," John broke in.

"Do you deny it?"

"I'm not discussing it."

"You must know, Mr. Graham, that the organisation is doomed, and that you are in an extremely dangerous position. I trust you realise this?"

"Quite warm last night, General!"

"Come, come, young man, I'm your friend—"

"It's a pleasure to meet a friend; do you think it will rain?"

"You are to be put on trial for your life——"

"My idea is that we are in for a long dry spell, General."

"Tut, tut, my boy, come now, don't try my temper with such nonsense. President Grant is not hostile to the South. He grieves over the necessity of the severe laws which he is now enforcing. His only desire is to pacify these disorders. The Klan must be stamped out. You have realised this—I know that you have led parties who have inflicted summary justice on some of the scoundrels who are operating in its disguises. Is not this a fact?"

John laughed.

"I know it," affirmed the General.

"Then why ask me?"

"I know that you have tried to stamp out the disorders," the General repeated. "Whatever the impulses which led a man of your high character into this lawless conspiracy, you have realised at last its dangerous character. You are in a position to render the South and the Nation an enormous service. Help me to restore law and order in the South and the Government will show its gratitude."

"You mean exactly?"

"That you give me the information needed to wipe the Invisible Empire out of existence——"

"And in return?"

The General placed his hands on the bars and leaned close.

"The President has promised me to immediately appoint you an Assistant Prosecuting Attorney, and in six months promote you to the high honour of a United States Circuit Judgeship."

John's fist suddenly shot through the iron bars, struck the General in the mouth, and hurled him in a heap against the wall of the corridor, as he cried with rage:

"D—— you! How dare you thus insult me?"

The General picked up his broken glasses from the floor, wiped a drop of blood from his lip, shook his fist at the man who glared at him through the barred door, and shouted:

"I'll make you pay dearly for this!"

John laughed in his face.

"But you won't make me that offer again, will you?"

CHAPTER III

A WOMAN'S WAY

IT WAS one o'clock before Stella recovered from the first collapse of terror for the fate of her lover. And then the imperious will summoned every energy to the struggle for his liberty and life.

She changed her riding habit and, taking Maggie, started at half past one in the morning to find Ackerman.

She had gone half way to Mrs. Wilson's before she recalled the startling fact that her relations to Ackerman were unknown, and the still more painful fact that all knowledge of her relations to the detective must now be concealed with the utmost care. She felt instinctively that if John Graham discovered her plan to entrap him into a confession and her betrayal of his generous trust in her love, he could not forgive it. She shivered at the thought of his anger and disgust.

"We'll go to the jail, Maggie," she said, with sudden energy, "where is it?"

"Right down de nex street, I show ye," Maggie answered. "I been dar lots er times. I wuz down dar yistiddy ter see my uncle Joe start ter de penitentiary."

Stella shuddered, followed her down the side street, and knocked at the jail door.

No one answered. She knocked again and again. Finally the jailor thrust his head from the window above, saw it was a woman, shut the sash with a bang and went back to bed.

Stella looked at the grim walls with a sense of blind fury.

"I'll show that insolent lazy rascal to-morrow morning how to treat me," she cried, as she turned and started home. When they reached the corner she stopped, looked back at the jail looming black, silent and threatening among the shadows, and her heart went out in an agony of piteous yearning to the man within its walls.

Maggie pointed to the mass of trees behind the jail.

"See dem trees dar behin' de house?"

Her mistress gave no answer, and the maid rattled on in awed whispers:

"Dars where dey hang folks! Dey's er high fence roun' de yard, but ye can see over it from here. I stan' right on dis corner an' see 'em hang a man dar las' year."

"Hush Maggie!" Stella sternly commanded.

"Yassum."

Stella hurried home, and paced the floor of her room until morning.

At eight o'clock, in answer to her urgent summons, Ackerman came.

"You are sure no one saw you enter?" she asked nervously.

"Yes, but why such caution now? Our work is done, and well done. I congratulate you on the skill with which you did your part."

"I had nothing to do with it. I've sent for you to have the whole thing stopped at once."

"You had nothing to do with it!" Ackerman exclaimed.

"Absolutely nothing. I repudiate the whole affair."

"I came here to do this work at your own request," he protested.

"The arrest of Mr. Graham is an infamous outrage!"

"What!"

"An infamous outrage. I repeat it and demand his immediate release."

"Why, my dear young woman, it was on the information which you gave that I swore out the warrant for his arrest."

"It was you who swore out the warrant against him?" Stella fiercely cried. "Oh, I could kill you!"

"You gave me the information."

"I did nothing of the kind," she stormed. It's false—I deny it!"

"On your statement to me that he had confessed that he was Chief of the Klan, I made the oath on which his warrant was based," Ackerman maintained with warmth.

"Then you swore a lie!" she hissed. "A lie— a lie!"

Stella fell on the lounge and buried her face in her hands.

Ackerman flushed and was silent. His keen eyes grew suddenly tender. He smiled, rose and stood by her side a moment, and when she looked up extended his hand.

"I'm sorry for you, Miss Stella. I think I understand!"

"Then you will know how to forgive my bitter and unjust words?"

"Yes."

"Can't you help me?" she asked piteously.

"The situation is extremely delicate for me as it is dangerous for John Graham. The Government is determined to press these cases for conspiracy and murder. Personally I have never believed Graham guilty of the murder of the Judge."

"Of course he is innocent!"

"I think I know the man who killed your father."

"And you will help me save John Graham?"
she cried.

"I'll have a big job before me to complete my
work before this trial. There'll be plenty of
witnesses to swear anything the Government wants,
but I'll do my best."

"Thank you."

With a cordial grasp of the hand Ackerman
took his leave and Stella hastened to confer with
the Attorney General.

"I've come to demand the immediate release of
Mr. Graham on the absurd charge that has been
made against him," she began impetuously.

The General looked at her in astonishment.
"Hoity toity! My dear Miss, not so fast."

"You began this at my request. I demand
that it cease."

"Yes, yes, I see, but you have forgotten that
greater issues are at stake than even the lives of
two men."

"I'll have nothing to do with the prosecution of
an innocent man, General Champion."

"Even so, you have set in motion forces you can
not control. The fate of Mr. Graham is fixed.
He is the Chief of the Klan. He's as sure of conviction as the fact that he is to be put on trial.
I'll see that he is tried and that all the resources of
the Government are used to secure his conviction."

Stella's beautiful face grew white and still.

"You will make a special effort against him ?" she faltered.

"I will," was the stern answer. "There was a way of escape. I offered it to him this morning in the most friendly and generous spirit. His answer was the gravest personal insult."

"May I see him at once ?"

"Certainly."

The General hastily wrote an order and Stella hurried to the jail.

She determined to make a desperate appeal to induce him to compromise with the authorities and save his life.

At the sight of the heavy iron bars of his door before which John stood smiling, she broke completely down, seized his extended hand, covered it with kisses and sobbed bitterly.

"Come, come, my beautiful one, this is not like you! I've counted on your brave spirit to win this fight. Not another tear. Courage and laughter in our souls, defiance, scorn, contempt for our enemies! See, they have made me quite comfortable within the past hour. I tried to knock the Attorney General down, and lo, they rewarded me with a cot and a chair!"

"You knocked General Champion down?" Stella gasped in amazement.

"I did my best under difficulties. Think of it, my dear! He offered me an office for the betrayal of my people! I couldn't kill him. I was behind the bars, but I shall always thank God that he stood close enough for my fist to reach his mouth."

John broke into a joyous laugh. His spirit was contagious. Stella looked at him with wonder until a smile stole through the clouds that shadowed her own brow.

"How beautiful you are this morning, dearest!" he cried exultantly.

She brushed the tears from her eyes.

"I tried to see you last night at two o'clock," she softly said.

"And succeeded, my love," he interrupted smiling. "You came up and stood there and talked to me just as you are now. You told me to be of good cheer—that you loved me. That you hated a sneak and a coward and a traitor. That you had rather see me cold in death than stoop to a low dishonourable deed, even for all the honours of earth. And I lifted up my head in courage. I forgot jails and handcuffs, courts and trials. You took me by the hand and led me away into green fields through the deep woods beside beautiful waters. All night hand in hand we roamed through the mystic world of Love— the only world of realities—I was angry with the sun for waking me!"

"My darling, I'm not worthy of such love," Stella cried, pressing his hand. "What can I do to help you?"

"Keep on loving me—that's the main thing!— incidentally consult a lawyer—the best you can find—tell him that I'm going to fight, fight, fight to the last ditch my own cause and the cause of my people! Keep out of old Champion's way. He carries a bribe in one hand, a death warrant in the other. Don't let him know your plans. Don't let him know that you love me."

Stella lifted her head with sudden resolution.

"I'll get the best lawyer in America. I'll mortgage the house for the money."

"My little heroine!" he exclaimed with pride.

"I'll go at once."

Through the iron bars she pressed her lips and hurried to the telegraph office with the light of new courage shining in her eyes.

CHAPTER IV

THE HON. STEPHEN HOYLE

STEVE HOYLE was confined to his room with a bullet hole through the flesh of his right arm the day following the meeting at Inwood.

He wrote Stella a letter informing her that John Graham had hired a gang of thugs to attempt his assassination on the night he was to meet her, that he had been desperately wounded in her service, and begged that she call at once.

Stella sent him a reply that cut deeper than the bullet from John's revolver. It was very brief. Steve read it with muttered curses:

MR. STEPHEN HOYLE,
I have long suspected that you were a liar. Last night you proved yourself a coward. Our acquaintance has ended.
STELLA BUTLER.

Steve paced his room in a speechless rage for an hour, dressed to call on her and demand an interview, and suddenly changed his mind at the sight of a squad of troops hurrying past his door.

The arrest of John Graham had brought him to the verge of collapse. He trembled at the thought that his turn might come next, and feared to put his head out the door.

. When ten minutes later the soldiers who had passed suddenly appeared at every exit of his house and loudly knocked for entrance, he dropped into a chair shivering with abject terror.

When arrested he turned his heavy white face toward the sergeant piteously.

"I beg of you, officer, allow me to stay here under guard.   I am desperately wounded, by an accident."

"You'll have to go to jail," the trooper snapped.

"But, my dear man, I can't.   I can't walk," he gasped with laboured breath.   "Just let me stay here under arrest until I can arrange with the authorities to give bail."

"Ye'll have ter fix that at headquarters—come on," he answered gruffly, seizing Steve and lifting him to his feet.

The heavy form collapsed and he sank in a heap on the floor.

The sergeant looked at him a moment with contempt, turned to his men and said:

"Keep him under guard till I report."

The moment he had gone, Steve revived and crawled in bed, his teeth chattering with a nervous chill.   The soldiers sat down and laughed in his face, and cracked jokes about the bravery of men who could ride well at night but sometimes fainted in the daylight.

The Attorney General had ordered Steve's arrest on a shrewd guess which Ackerman had made on hearing of the strange fight between two groups of horsemen in the country at dusk the night before. The detective had seen the doctor leaving Hoyle's house and learned at once that Steve was wounded.

In attempting to serve the warrant on John Graham he had found that he had ridden into the country alone in the direction taken by Steve Hoyle. Ackerman had long suspected Steve of complicity in the movements of the Klan, and knowing the deadly enmity between the two men had at once reached the conclusion that a feud within the ranks of its members could alone account for the situation.

"Arrest Hoyle," he urged on Champion; "threaten him with immediate conviction for conspiracy and murder and see what happens."

The Attorney General had taken his advice, and on receiving the report of Steve's "illness" from the sergeant, went immediately to see him.

Steve was profuse in his expressions of cordiality.

"I'm sorry, General Champion," he said, with loud friendliness, "that my father and mother are in the North at present. They spend a great deal

of their time up there among you good Yankees.
The fact is they are specially fond of you. My
father, you know, was a secret Union man during
the war and has always voted your ticket since,
though for social reasons he don't say much about
it down here."

Steve winked and laughed feebly.

"Is it so?" asked the General.

"Yes, of course," Steve hurried on, "and I
want to ask you as a personal favour to my father,
if not to me, to accept my bail for $10,000. The
whole thing, I assure you, is an absurd mistake.
My father and I can convince you of this on his
return."

The General pursed his lips and watched Steve
shrewdly for a moment.

"I'm sorry I can't accommodate you, Mr. Hoyle.
We cannot accept bail in cases of this kind. You
must realise at once that you are in a very dangerous position. Beyond a doubt your life is in
peril."

Steve attempted to laugh but choked with
terror, saying feebly:

"Oh, not so bad as that, General. I'm a lawyer
myself you know. I can only be tried on a charge
of murder before a state judge and jury. You
have no right to put a man on trial for his life
here."

"Right or no right, young man, we are going to do it under the Act of Congress. We've got the power. The army is here. The Supreme Court may decide the Act unconstitutional later."

"I assure you, General, the charge against me is a monstrous falsehood," Steve protested vigorously.

"And yet, my boy, the men have found in the search of this house a full Ku Klux regalia for man and horse. Sergeant, bring that thing in!"

The trooper stepped in the door and held up before Steve's astonished gaze the costume which he had taken under his saddle the night before on his trip to meet Stella.

Steve sat up in bed trembling and perspiring.

"Why, yes, of course," he stammered. "That has been here for some time. I've made no attempt to conceal it. It was given me by a client of mine who was a member. I'm keeping it as a curiosity."

"A dangerous curiosity to keep about your house in these times, sir," said the General sternly. "Let's come to the point. Do you wish to keep out of jail or do you wish to test the power of the United States Government to put you on trial for your life?".

"I want to keep out of jail," was the quick answer.

"That's sensible. Then face the facts. My detective has watched you for three months. I can convict you of murder."

Steve fumbled his hands nervously while the General paused and gazed steadily at his wavering eyes.

"Now, I've a generous proposition to make you."

"Yes ?—yes ?" Steve gasped.

"One that will give you an opportunity to prove yourself a patriot and a hero—a patriot because you will render your country a great service—a hero because you must brave the scorn of every white man and woman whose opinion is worth anything to you. Will you consider it ?"

"Yes," Steve answered.

"Give me the information needed to destroy the Invisible Empire and I will not only release you from custody; I will make you my assistant and ultimately secure your promotion to a judgeship. Your answer ?"

"I'll do it, General, I'll do it!" Steve cried, while the maudlin tears of a coward's relief from mortal fear coursed down his fat cheeks. I'll stand by you and help save our country by restoring law and order."

The General thanked and congratulated him, again called him a patriot and hero and sent for his stenographer.   For four hours he was closeted with Steve.

At dusk the soldiers moved with sure tread in every county in Piedmont Carolina, and before the sun rose the blow had fallen swift, relentless, terrible!

The Klan leaders in every county were behind the bars.

More than five hundred arrests were made in the county of Independence.   Around the jail, and half a dozen improvised prisons, throngs of sad-faced wives, mothers, sisters and sweethearts stood silently weeping.

The next morning Champion wired the President asking that the Honourable Stephen Hoyle be appointed acting Assistant United States District Attorney, and his request was granted.

CHAPTER V

ACKERMAN CORNERED

THE arrest of John Graham precipitated a crisis between Ackerman and Susie Wilson which was as unexpected as it was embarrassing to the handsome young detective.

From the moment she had seen his letter on Stella's bed she had watched the young Northerner with the keenest suspicions.

The following day he pressed his love with straightforward earnestness.

She answered with an evasive smile.

"I appreciate the honour you pay me, Mr. Ackerman, but I'm not in love with you. I hope we shall always be friends. If your love endures it may win mine in the end—if you persist."

"I have your permission to persist?"

"Certainly," she answered frankly. "I love to be loved."

"All right," he said with a boyish laugh. "I'm going to build my house in the fall."

On the day following John Graham's arrest she saw Ackerman emerge from the hotel in earnest consultation with the Attorney General. To her the prosecuting officer of the United States at that moment meant all that was vile and hateful in the tyranny under which the South had groaned since the dawn of her memory. The moment she saw Ackerman with this man, his very name became to her accursed. Her keen intuition at once linked the letter to Stella with the murder of the Judge and the prosecution of the Klan. She was sure that Ackerman had been playing the hypocrite and was at heart an enemy of the South. She determined not only to cut his acquaintance but put him out of her mother's house.

When the young detective received a written notice from Susie to vacate his room immediately, he took it to be a practical joke and asked to see her. She sent word by the servant that unless he moved during the day his trunk would be thrown on the sidewalk.

Ackerman left in answer to a summons from the Attorney General's office, still puzzling his brain over the meaning of the joke. He was sure that she could not possibly know of his oath against John Graham which was a secret of the Department of Justice. He was equally sure that she could not suspect his real business in Independence. He meant to win her love first. He didn't care what she thought of his profession afterwards.

When he returned to Mrs. Wilson's for supper he was struck dumb by the sight of his trunk lying on the sidewalk outside the gate.

Without a word he picked it up, carried it back upstairs and threw it on the floor with a bang in front of the room that had been his.

He sat down on it and refused to stir until Susie answered in person his demand for an interview.

To avoid a scene she finally consented to meet him in the parlour.

Susie's gray eyes were cold and her tall figure rigid.

"In violation of every law that should govern the conduct of a gentleman you have forced yourself into my presence Mr. Ackerman.   I trust our interview may be very brief."

"In violation of every law of Southern hospitality, to say nothing of the rules which should govern the temper of a lady, you have thrown me out of your house without rhyme or reason.   And before I go I respectfully but firmly ask, why?"

"You have pretended to be a friend of our people I find that you are an enemy—a sneak and a hypocrite."

Ackerman's cheeks blushed redder than usual; he bit his lips and finally burst into laughter.

"Is that all?"

Susie rose with dignity.

"It's quite enough for my mother and myself."

"But it's not enough for me, Miss Susie. My defence against your unjust suspicions is perfect. I will make it if necessary. I trust it will not be necessary."

"You might include in your defence an explanation of why you were corresponding with Stella Butler while you were writing love to me?"

"Who said that I wrote to Miss Butler?"

"I say it. I saw your letter in her room the day you declared your love for me."

Ackerman was cornered. He must confess and betray Stella's secret or keep silent and wreck his own hopes. His decision was instantly made.

"Miss Susie, you've got me. I give up. I'm not a sneak—but I am a hypocrite by profession."

"You confess it?" Susie cried with scorn.

"Yes," he whispered. "I am a trusted detective of the United States Secret Service. I am not the enemy of your people. On the other hand, I have learned to love and sympathise with them. Perhaps my love for you has given me that point of view. Anyway, I've taken it. I am simply here as an officer on duty under command of his superior."

Susie's face softened. She saw at once her mistake.

"And your duty led you into correspondence with Miss Butler?"

"I regret to be compelled to answer, but it did."

"She has aided in your work?"

"Yes. I reported to her by order of the Chief on arrival, and have been in constant communication with her at every step since."

"Up to the hour of John Graham's arrest?" Susie asked breathlessly.

"Yes."

"Oh, the little fiend! I could strangle her!" the girl cried.

"I'm sorry to have to betray this confidence. But you have forced me."

"And you are pressing the charge of murder against John Graham?"

"On the other hand, I am not. If my plans succeed, I'll explode a bombshell in the court room the day he faces the jury."

Susie extended her hand.

"I beg your pardon for my rudeness. Alfred will put your trunk back immediately, if you will stay."

Ackerman mounted to his room and unpacked his trunk, humming a love song while Susie put on her hat and left with swift firm step to find Stella Butler.

CHAPTER VI

STELLA had hurried to the jail with a bouquet
of flowers earlier than usual, accompanied
by Maggie who carried a dainty breakfast. She
wished to be the first to tell John Graham of the
blow which had fallen on his people. She had
forgotten that the jail in which he lay had been
jammed with prisoners during the night. Four
of his friends were crowded into the cell in which
he was confined.

Her heart sank at the sight of the pitiful crowds
of weeping women who stood at the jail door,
some of them with sick babies in their arms.

A little tow-headed boy sat on the steps, with
his lips quivering and the big tears slowly rolling
down his cheeks. She recognised him as the one
she saw in front of her house the night of the
Klan's first parade.

She bent over him and took his hand:

"What's the matter?"

The boy's breast heaved and he choked, unable
to answer, bent his sunburnt head on Stella's
hand and burst into strangling tears.

She stroked his hair, and at length he sobbed:

"They've got my big brother in here—locked—up—in—a—cage! They're going to kill him, and he ain't got nobody but me to help him. I ain't nothing but a little boy. I can't get no money, and I can't do nothing. Oh, me! oh, me!"

He bowed again and sobbed as though his heart would break.

Stella slipped her arm around his neck and placed a rose in his hand.

"Hush dear, I'll be your friend and his. I've got money. I'll help you—give the rose to your brother and come to see me."

"Will you, Miss?" he cried, leaping up with joy. "Make 'em let me go in with you and I'll tell him!"

Stella took him by the hand and led him into the jail.

When the jailor frowned at the boy, she said with a smile:

"He's a little friend of mine. He'll go in with me."

The boy nestled close to her side and gripped her hand tightly. When they reached the first corridor, he sprang to a grated door and seized his brother's hand. As she passed on Stella heard him say joyously:

"It'll be all right, Jim, don't worry. She's a

goin' to help us. She told me so. She's rich—
she'll get us a lawyer."

Stella climbed the stairs to John's door with a
great voiceless fear in her soul. The thought of
his discovery of her betrayal stopped the very
beat of her heart.

To her surprise she found him strangely calm.

"It's sweet of you to come so early," he said
with a smile.

"Love makes one's feet swift, doesn't it?" she
answered softly.

"And beautiful!" he cried. "I'm going to
make you happier by giving you more work.
Don't bring me anything more to eat or any more
flowers until you've made the other fellows comfortable. I'm all right, but a lot of the poor boys
who have just come have broken down. Oh,
God, if I could have gotten my hands on the
throat of the traitor last night!"

Never had she seen a more terrible look on a
human face. Stella gazed at his convulsed
features fascinated with fear.

"You'll help the boys, won't you, dear, for my
sake?" he asked suddenly. "Susie Wilson and
her mother will join you."

Stella answered with a start:

"Why—of course, John. I'll go at once."

"And dear!" he called as she turned quickly.

"The lawyer whom you engage for me must take all their cases. I'll stand or fall with my people."

"Yes, I understand."

Stella hurried home with her soul in a tumult of conflicting purposes. She felt it yet too dangerous to confess the dual rôle she had played; yet with each hour's startling events the agony of fear lest he discover her betrayal became more and more intense.

One thing she could do at once. She would make the cause of his men her own, she would make her ministry of love so tender and unselfish, her sacrifices so generous he must hear her plea when the awful moment of her confession should come.

She had just given Aunt Julie Ann orders to prepare three meals each day for every man in jail with John, and was about to start for the garden to cut more flowers, when Maggie ushered Susie Wilson into the hall.

"I'm so glad you've come," Stella cried. "I was just going to ask you and your mother to help us make those men comfortable who have been put in jail. Mr. Graham was sure you would join me."

Susie stared at Stella for a moment and slowly said:

"Is it possible!"

"Why, what's the matter?" Stella asked. "Won't you sit down?"

"I prefer to stand, thank you, and to come straight to the point," Susie answered with quiet emphasis. "May I ask you some questions?"

Stella flushed and her first impulse was to show her questioner to the door, but she felt the dangerous menace in Susie's tone and knew that she had suspected at least part of the truth. It was necessary to fence.

"Why, as many as you like," she replied with a light laugh.

"You have told John Graham that you love him?"

"Your question is an impertinence. It's none of your business."

"I have made it my business."

"Then the sooner you recover your self-respect the better," Stella sneered.

"What do you mean?" Susie's gray eyes danced with anger.

"That you are desperately and hopelessly in love with John Graham yourself, and that you haven't pride and character enough to hold up your head before his indifference, and his patronising contempt. I have won him, and you come with cheap insults for the woman he loves."

Susie's eyes grew dim.

"Your accusation is infamously false," she cried with choking emotion.

"You deny that you love him?" Stella flashed.

"I glory in it—if you will know!" Susie cried in dreamy tenderness. "I've always loved him with a girl's blind worship of the hero of her dreams. And I shall cherish every gentle word that he has ever spoken to me. The impulse which brought me here wasn't the vulgar desire to insult the woman he loves. I came to save his life."

Stella sprang to her feet, her face scarlet, her breath coming in quick gasps of anger.

"What do you mean?"

"I'll tell you if you answer my questions. Do you dare tell me that you love him?"

Stella drew herself up proudly.

"You have no right to ask that question. But I answer it. I do love him and I have told him."

Susie confronted her with flashing eyes.

"Then you have deceived him!"

"How dare you thus insult me in my house," Stella cried with flaming cheeks.

"I'll leave your house and never enter it again. You can also rest assured that John Graham's foot will never again cross this threshold when I have told him the truth."

"When — you — have — told — him — the — truth!" Stella gasped. "What truth?"

"That you have betrayed him and his people to his enemies."

"It's false! It's false!" Stella panted. "You lie. You lie, because you hate me! You hate me because you love him. Tell him if you dare. He will laugh in your face! Try it—try it—I dare you!" Her voice rose and fell, quivering and breaking in hoarse whispers of passion.

Susie stood quietly and coldly staring at her with lips upturned in scorn.

"If he doubts my word, Mr. Ackerman's will be sufficient."

"Ackerman!" Stella moaned, staggering to the table.

"Mr. Ackerman of the Secret Service who came here in answer to your call."

"He—has—told—you?"

"Yes, and I know the whole black hideous truth. I know that you hate John Graham, that you have used your devil's beauty to entrap and betray him."

"I swear that I love him!" Stella groaned as she sank to a chair.

"As you've sworn to him no doubt while you lured him to his ruin. I hate you—I hate you—and I could strangle you!"

The tall lithe form trembling with fury towered above Stella's shivering little figure.

"Susie, you are mistaken," she faltered. "Come into the library a moment and I'll convince you that you are wrong."

She seized Susie's hand and led her into the library, sinking again into a chair.

"See, here is a mortgage for ten thousand dollars on this house which I've prepared to raise the money for two great lawyers from the North who are coming to defend him."

"From the North?"

"Yes."

"You mean to convict him," Susie cried. "Another shrewd trick you are playing. Your lawyers will gain his confidence, learn his secrets, betray and send him to his death. But, I'll warn him!"

"Susie, you can't believe this of me! The pledging of this house is the first great act of self-sacrifice of my life. The joy of it has been a sweet revelation to me. You must hear me when I tell you that I love him with passionate devotion. I'd give my life for him if I could!"

"And yet you brought Ackerman here and hounded him for three months until at last he lies in a filthy jail with the shadow of death over him—and you call this love?"

The tall form again towered in rage above the shrinking figure.

"Wait! I must tell you all, Susie. You know but half the truth. Listen dear, I did try to avenge my father's death. I believed John Graham guilty. I did lure him on to love me only to find that I loved him! I tried to hate him and couldn't. I've betrayed only his name to Ackerman. I could tear my tongue out for it. If he learns of it, he will turn from me and hate me! Susie darling, I've been proud and vain and wilful. Now I'm a poor little girl alone, friendless and lost. You're stronger than I am. Have pity on me. Be a mother to me—I'm lonely and heart-sick. You know what it is to love. If he turns from me now before I can atone for the wrong I have done him, I can't live. You—believe—me—now—dear?"

Susie's eyes filled with tears.

"Yes, I believe you now."

Stella's head sank on the table and her form shook with sobs.

Susie gently stroked the curling black hair, and said:

"I'll help you. We'll work together to save his life."

In a moment they were sobbing in each other's arms.

CHAPTER VII

THE PRISONER AT THE BAR

WHEN the day of trial dawned, Stella had succeeded in securing the services of two of the greatest lawyers in America, Reverdy Johnson of Maryland, Attorney General in the Cabinet of President Taylor, and Henry Stanbery of Ohio, Attorney General in the Cabinet of Andrew Johnson.

The Government was represented by the finest legal talent its vast resources and power could command.

For eleven days, before two presiding judges of the United States Circuit Court, the fierce battle of legal giants raged. The great lawyers for the defence fought every inch of ground with dogged tenacity.

Stella watched from day to day with breathless intensity as she sat by John Graham's side.

It soon became plain that the Court had constituted itself a partisan political tribunal for the purpose, not of administering justice, but of crushing the enemies of the party in power.

Every decision was against the prisoner, though,

in deference to the distinguished character of the lawyers for the defence, they were allowed to argue each point. The profound and accurate learning with which they reviewed the Constitutional law of the Republic was a liberal education to the shallow little partisans who sat on the judge's bench before them. But their eloquence and learning fell on the ears of men whose decisions were already made.

In violation of the rights of the prisoner under the constitutions of the state and nation the indictment for murder was ordered to immediate trial.

From the moment the actual proceedings of the trial began, the Government had no delay or difficulty.

With sinking heart Stella saw the disgraceful travesty of justice draw each moment the cords of death closer about the form of the man she loved.

The jury corruptly chosen for this case marked the lowest tide mud to which the administration of justice ever sank in our history. A white freeman, a man of culture and heroic mould, whose fathers created the American Republic, was arraigned to plead for his life before a jury composed of one dirty, ignorant white scalawag and eleven coal-black Negroes! The white man was not made its foreman, a Negro teamster was chosen.

Steve Hoyle became at once the presiding genius of the prosecution. The court room was thronged with liars, perjurers and sycophants who hung about his fat figure with obsequious deference. Old Larkin, who came from the Capitol to assist the prosecution, sat constantly by Steve's side.

John Graham watched Steve with cold deadly hate, but he had warned his men under no conceivable circumstances to lift a hand in resistance either to constituted authority, or to give the traitor his deserts. A pall of helpless grief and fear hung over every decent white man who witnessed the High Court of Justice of the Anglo-Saxon race suddenly transformed into a Negro minstrel farce on which hung their liberty and life.

The star witness of the prosecution was Uncle Isaac A. Postle. He took his seat before the jury, grinning and nodding at two of his dusky friends among them with calm assurance.

Isaac was allowed to tell a marvellous rambling story of Ku Klux outrages—stories which he had heard from Larkin—about whose truth he could possibly know nothing. In vain the lawyers for the defence objected. The court overruled every objection and allowed the Apostle free scope to his vivid imagination.

Reverdy Johnson, the distinguished ex-Attorney General of the United States who stood before the judges protesting with dignity, bowed to the Bench and sat down in disgust with the quiet remark:

"We shall offer no further objection to anything that may be said in this Court."

He had scarcely taken his seat when Ackerman moved his chair behind him and began to whisper.

The District Attorney watched the detective in astonishment, while Hoyle and Larkin bent their heads together in excited conference.

Susie looked at Stella, smiled and blushed.

Isaac finally came to specific charges against John Graham.

"Now tell the court what you know about John Graham's connection with the murder of Judge Butler," said Steve, who was conducting his examination.

"Yassah, I knows all 'bout it, sah. Mr. John Graham de very man dat kill de jedge wid his own han'. I see 'im when he do it. Dey come slippin' up back er de house, an' creep in froo de winder while de odder folks wuz in de ballroom dancin'. Dey wuz eight un 'em—yassah. Dey slip up an' grab de jedge an' hol' 'im while Mr. John Graham stick a knife right in his heart——yassah. I wuz lookin' right at 'im froo de winder when he done it. When he kill 'im, dey all mix up wid de odder Ku Kluxes what wuz dancin', an' go way ter-gedder."

"Take the witness," said Steve with a wave of his hand.

"How did you know it was Mr. Graham?" asked General Johnson.

"I seed 'im wid my own eyes."

"He wore a complete disguise, did he not?"

"Yassah, but I seed 'im all de same."

"You could see through the mask?"

"I seed 'im—I done tole ye!"

"Answer my question," sternly commanded the lawyer. "Could you see his face through the mask?"

"Nasah."

"Then how did you recognise him?"

"He tuck it off ter scratch his head, sah, an' I see his face. I knowed it wuz him all de time fo' I see his face."

Ackerman whispered to the lawyer.

"Did you tell Mr. Ackerman, Uncle Isaac, that, as you started to run away from the masqueraders that night, you saw John Graham at your gate— ran into him?"

"Nasah, I nebber say no sech thing!" Isaac shouted, glaring and shaking his head at Ackerman.

"Didn't you tell the same gentleman that later in the evening you saw John Graham seated on a rustic near the house watching it from the outside?"

"Nasah! dat I didn't!"

"Do you know that if you swear a lie——"

"I ain't swar no lie!" Isaac interrupted with religious fervour. "I'se de Lord's Sanctified One, sah. I ain't done no sin since I got sanctification. Yassah, praise God!"

"Don't you know," repeated the lawyer, "that if you swear to a lie on that witness stand you can be sent to the penitentiary for perjury?"

"I knows dey ain't gwine sen' me dar—I knows dat," Isaac said with a grin, and his Negro acquaintances in the jury box laughed.

The lawyer changed his line of questions.

"You say you saw John Graham strike the death-blow?"

"Yassah, I see 'im wid dese very eyes."

"Were you close enough to hear what was said?"

"Yassah, I wuz right dar by de open winder."

"What did he say?"

"Des ez he raise de knife he say, "I got you now, you d—— Black Radical 'Publican!"

"You swear that you heard him say that he killed the Judge because he was a Republican?"

"Yassah! dat's what de Ku Kluxes kill 'em all fur, sah!"

Larkin shuffled uneasily, bent again in conference with Steve who rose immediately and asked for an adjournment of two hours,

When the Court reassembled and Isaac took his seat in the witness chair, Aunt Julie Ann's huge form suddenly appeared in the doorway with her hand resting confidingly on Alfred's arm. They walked inside the railing of the bar and took seats assigned to them behind John Graham's counsel. Aunt Julie Ann handed Ackerman a pair of Isaac's old shoes. He measured them quickly on a diagram which he drew from his pocket.

Isaac watched Aunt Julie Ann and Alfred with mouth opened in wonder, rage and growing fear.

He rose and bowed to the judges.

"I gotter ax de cote ter perteck me, gemmens," he said falteringly.

"What do you mean?" asked a judge.

"Dat nigger Alfred dar tryin' ter steal my wife from me, sah!"

Alfred grinned, and patted Aunt Julie Ann's hand and whispered: "Doan min' de low-live rascal, honey!"

"Yassah, an' my wife come here tryin' ter 'timidate me, sah. She jes fetch er par er my ole shoes inter dis cote. She's a cunjer 'oman, sah. I try ter sanctify her, but she won't stay sanctified. She got a kink er my hair las' night and wrap it up in a piece er paper and put it under de cote house do' step, an' she say dat ef I walk

over dat into dis house ter-day an' jestify ergin
Marse John Graham she fling er spell over me.
I ax de cote fer pertection, sah.   I axes de Sheriff
ter take dat bunch er hair from under dem steps
fo' I say annuder word!"

"Silence, sir, and proceed with your testimony,"
said the Judge.

Aunt Julie Ann fanned her fat face, smiled at
Stella and Susie and quietly slipped her hand in
Alfred's.

Isaac dropped into his chair limp and crest-
fallen.   In a sort of dazed trance he kept his eye
fixed on Alfred's face grinning in triumph.

John's lawyer pounced on him in sudden sharp
accents.

"Is this a pair of your shoes, Isaac?"

"Yassah," was the listless answer.

"You wore these shoes the night the Judge was
killed, didn't you?"

"Yassah."

"You're sure of it?"

"Yassah.   Dem's my ole ones.   I got a new
pair now."

The lawyer stepped close and in threatening
tones asked:

"Will you explain to this Court what your
shoes were doing making tracks in the soft
mud of the underground passage from the family

vault of the Graham house the night of this murder?"

Isaac's jaw dropped, he drew his red bandanna handkerchief and mopped his brow.

A hum of excitement ran over the court room, and an officer cried:

"Silence!"

Isaac continued to mop his brow and fumble at his handkerchief while he gazed at the lawyer in a helpless stupor.

"Answer my question, sir!" the towering figure thundered into his face.

"I doan know what yer means, sah," he faltered.

"Yes you do. There were nine other men with you. Who were they?"

"I dunno, sah!"

Larkin whispered excitedly to Steve, who shook his head and gazed at Isaac in amazement.

"Were they masked so that you couldn't see their faces?"

Isaac looked appealingly to the judges and whimpered:

"I doan know what dey er talkin' 'bout, sah."

"You must answer the questions," said the Judge.

The lawyer glared at Isaac whose shifting eyes sought Larkin.

"Think it over a minute, Isaac," the lawyer continued; "in the meantime examine that knife."

He drew from its case a long, keen hunting-knife, and handed it to the witness who was now trembling from head to foot.

"Did you ever see that knife before?"

Isaac hesitated and finally answered:

"Yassah, I sold it ter Mr. Ackerman."

"Where did you get it?"

Larkin suddenly cleared his throat with a deep guttural sound like the growl of an infuriated animal.

The lawyer looked at him with annoyance and the officer again shouted:

"Silence!"

"I foun' it, sah," he answered evasively.

"Now, Isaac, you want to be very careful how you answer my next question."

The lawyer took the knife from the Negro's hand and felt of its point.

"You will notice that a tiny piece is broken off the tip of this blade. I hold in my hand the little bit of steel which exactly fits there. It was found embedded in a bone in Judge Butler's body. This is the knife that struck the death-blow. Did you own that knife the night of the murder? Answer me!"

Isaac fumbled his handkerchief again and looked about the room helplessly.

Larkin rose carelessly and started from the

court room. Ackerman, watching him keenly, sprang to his side.

"Don't leave, Larkin, we want you as a witness in a moment," he whispered.

"I'll return immediately," the Carpetbagger replied, increasing his haste.

"Wait!" Ackerman commanded.

Larkin quickened his pace and the detective seized his arm.

The Carpetbagger threw him off with sudden fury and plunged toward the door.

With the spring of a tiger, Ackerman leaped on him. A brief fierce fight, and he was dragged panting back before the astonished Court, while every man in the room sprang to his feet and pressed around the struggling men.

"What's the meaning of this disorder?" thundered the presiding Judge.

"With apologies to the Court for the interruption I beg leave to present the murderer of Judge Butler—I ask a warrant for his arrest," Ackerman demanded.

A wave of horror swept the crowd of Larkin's friends.

"The man is a crazy liar, your Honours," protested Larkin. "And he has proven himself a renegade and a scoundrel in this court room to-day. I protest against this outrage."

"I'll prove my charge to the Court—every link in the chain of evidence is now complete," was the cool answer.

With the court room in an uproar, Larkin was arrested and placed between Ackerman and a deputy, and the trial resumed.

A brief conference between the District Attorney and Isaac preceded the first question asked by John's counsel after the disturbance.

"Now, Isaac," the lawyer began suavely, "the District Attorney has just promised to spare your life on condition that you tell us the truth, the whole truth, and nothing but the truth—let's have it."

"Yassah," the Apostle responded in humble accents. "Mr. Larkin, he tell me ter say what I did, sah."

Larkin's head dropped and his keen eyes furtively sought the door.

"Who gave you that knife?"

A moment of breathless suspense rippled the crowded court room and every head was bent forward.

"Mr. Larkin gimme de knife! We'se been powful good friends, sah. I show him de undergroun' way fum de tomb inter de house. I'se de only black man dat know it—my daddy help dig it—yassah. Mr. Larkin de fust man I ebber tell dat I know 'bout it. He say he want ter beat de Ku Kluxes. He say he make 'em smoke dat night, an' he git eight men an' dress up jes lak 'em, an' I show him de way ter git in froo de panel in de hall. He fool me. I didn't know he gwine ter kill de jedge, sah, er I wouldn't er let 'em in, nosah. I doan' believe in killin' nobody. He tell me ter git outen de county an' I stay till de soldiers come back. Yassah, an' dat's de whole troof!"

Ackerman. motioned the sergeant, a pair of handcuffs clicked on Larkin's wrists, and the great white head sank on his breast.

Stella gazed at his pathetic figure with a strange feeling of pity and wonder, while her hand sought John Graham's and pressed it tenderly.

The count of murder was dropped, but the charge of conspiracy was pressed with merciless ferocity. A procession of hired liars ascended the witness stand and in rapid succession perjured themselves by swearing that they had recognised the prisoner on various raids made by the Klan in the county.

The jury was out fifteen minutes.

When they returned John Graham, in whose veins flowed the blood of a race of world-con-quering men, entitled to a trial by a jury of his peers, rose with quiet dignity and heard the verdict of his condemnation fall from the thick protruding lips of a flat-nosed Negro:

"We finds de prisoner guilty!"

"So say you all gentlemen?" asked the clerk.

And in response each black spindle-shanked juror shambled to his feet and answered:

"Guilty!"

The last name called was the little white Scala-wag's, whose weak voice squeaked an echo:

"Guilty."

The Judge imposed a fine of one thousand dollars and sentenced John Graham to five years imprisonment at hard labour in the United States penitentiary at Albany, New York.

A low moan from Stella, and her head sank in voiceless anguish.

To the brave and the proud there are visions darker than death.

John Graham saw this as he was led from the court room back to jail—the vision of the hideous leprous shame of a convict's suit of stripes!

CHAPTER VIII

THE MINISTRY OF ANGELS

EVERY delicacy which love could devise and her money buy Stella lavished on John and his friends. Each day added to the list of men who returned to jail condemned to the infamy of a convict's pen at Albany.

When the deep-muttered curses against Steve Hoyle for the betrayal of his men reached John's ears, he sent through Stella his sternest orders and his tenderest entreaties to Dan Wiley to prevent violence. Dan had successfully eluded every effort to arrest him. John knew that he was hiding in the mountains with the men he had commanded armed to the teeth, and he lived in constant dread of the news of Steve's assassination, even under the noses of the United States troops.

A single burst of sunlight came to brighten for Stella the gloom of the day before John's departure for Albany. She succeeded in liberating "Jim," the big brother of her little tow-headed friend. Her interest in the boy had been noted, and she received the usual mysterious message—that money placed at the right spot would prevent any witness

from identifying Jim. She found the right spot
promptly and paid the bribe of two hundred and
fifty dollars without a question as to the ethics
involved. Jim was discharged, and when he
walked out a free man a little tow-headed boy lay
sobbing out his joy on her breast.

"I'm goin' to work for you, if you'll let me,"
he cried through his tears.

"Why, I thought you said you couldn't do
anything that day we met?" she laughed.

"Oh, I'm awful smart," he boasted—"I can
tote fresh water, carry all your notes to your sweetheart—and I'm great diggin' worms ter go fishin'—
I know right where to find 'em!"

She sent him away with a kiss and a promise to
let him come and show her what he could do.

As she entered the jail with John's dinner, the
jailor, whose friendship she had won by the liberal
use of money and skilful flattery, whispered to her:

"Come in here a minute, Miss, I want to show
you something."

She followed him into his room and started with
horror at the sight of a dirty suit of convict's
stripes spread out on a chair.

Stella's face blanched.

"They are for him?" she gasped.

"Yessum, an' if ye'll excuse me fer sayin' it,
I think it's a d—— shame."

"They have no right to put this outrage on him before his people," she cried.

"No'm, they haint got no right, but they're goin' ter do it to-morrow mornin' just the same. They're goin' ter take him all the way ter Albany in that suit."

"Who's doing this?" she asked with rising wrath.

"Steve Hoyle, m'am. He's fixin' to have a big gang er niggers and low white trash here in the mornin' ter hoot and yell and make fun of him all the way to the train, an' I thought I'd tell ye."

"Thank you," she answered warmly, her big brown eyes beginning to flash fire.

"Ye know ef I'd step out, that suit o' clothes might be foun' missin'. It ain't mine. I'll swear to that. I don't know anybody that owns it, er wants it."

"I understand. Wrap it up, please. I can't touch it."

Stella shuddered and watched the jailor with wide-staring eyes as he picked up the suit, wrapped it in a piece of brown paper and laid it back on the chair.

"I got to go—there's somebody knockin' at the door—course, I won't know what's become er the d—— thing."

He left her with a grin, and Stella seized the

bundle, hurried home and burned it. On the way she stopped at a hardware store and made a mysterious purchase which she carefully concealed, and there was a dangerous light in her eyes as she placed this package beside the travelling dress which she had laid out to wear on the train with John.

The jailor passed Stella in the hall but looked the other way as he hurried forward with two soldiers who had called to see John Graham. They were dressed in the regulation blue suits of the army. The jailor, trusting implicitly their uniforms, allowed them to go up unaccompanied to John's door.

So complete was the disguise that at first the condemned man gazed through the bars with indifference at his callers.

The taller of the two suddenly thrust his face close and whispered:

"God, man, don't ye know me?"

John started.

"Dan—Billy—what does this mean!"

Dan put his finger on his lips.

"Everything's all right. Billy's been up in the mountains with me at my summer resort."

"I wrote you, Billy, not to come!" John scowled.

"I'm not going to see this infamy put on you——"

"It's all fixed, Chief," Dan broke in, drawing a

new sledge hammer from his pocket, and slipping the handle from his sleeve.

With a loud cough to mask the sound he thrust the handle into its place.

"You're both crazy!" John said with anger.

"It's as easy as fallin' off a log," Dan urged.

"Billy'll smash the lock, I'll gag and tie the jailor. I've got the fastest horse in the county waitin' fer ye at the corner. Git thirty minutes start, an' there ain't cavalry enough this side er hell to stop ye. When ye get ter my house, ye'll be in God's country. The boys are there waitin' fer ye."

Dan handed the hammer to Billy.

"Put that hammer down!" John commanded sternly.

"I won't—you've got to go with us."

"Do as I tell you, or I'll call the jailor," John said with a frown.

"For God's sake, come with us!" Billy pleaded. "Steve Hoyle's going to have a crowd of Negroes here to laugh and jeer at you to-morrow as you come out. I tell you I can't stand it!"

John's face suddenly paled.

"You can stand it if I can, Billy! Get out of this, both of you, before you're arrested—quick now. I won't have it. Come here, Dan!"

John called to the mountaineer who had turned away.

"Give me your hand."

Dan thrust his hand through the bars and John grasped it.

"Are you a friend of mine?"

"Ain't I a showin' ye."

"Take Billy home and take care of him until I return—will you do it?"

"Yes—but I don't like this givin' up a fight when I've won it."

"And one thing more, Dan, old boy, before I let your hand go, you've got to promise me not to kill Steve Hoyle."

"Who said I was goin' to do it?"

"I say it."

"He ain't fit ter live."

"Yes, but somehow God lets a lot of such trash cumber the earth. We'd better not try any more interference with his plans."

Dan hesitated, struggling with deep passion, drew a handkerchief and blew his nose.

"Ye're putty hard on me, Chief, I was goin' ter call by Steve's house and finish both jobs to-day, but orders is orders. I'll take 'em from you. I won't take 'em from nobody else. Good-bye, take care er yourself."

Billy pressed his brother's hand, silently turned and left with Dan.

When the last echo of their steps had died away

John Graham stared through the iron bars for half an hour and saw only the vision of a mob of yelling, laughing Negroes and behind them the fat, white cowardly face of Steve Hoyle.

He sank to the chair with a groan:

"O God, if it be possible let this cup pass from me!"

CHAPTER IX

THE DAY OF ATONEMENT

WHEN Steve Hoyle discovered next morning that the suit of stripes which he had secured at enormous expense in bribery and hush money had been lost he was furious. The jailor laughed at his idle threats and cursed him roundly when accused of making way with the suit.

Steve left in a rage to drum up a larger crowd to hoot and yell at the man he hated.

Stella pressed her way through the throng of Negroes into the jail, carrying an enormous bouquet of roses in one hand and in the other a basket of delicate flowers threaded into long beautiful garlands.

John determined to save her from the scene of his humiliation.

"You must not go through the streets with me to the train, my dear," he said tenderly. "Go down in a carriage and join me at the station."

"I will if they let you ride with me," she firmly answered.

"Impossible. They've given special orders that I shall walk."

"Then I'll walk with you," she said with a smile.

John's face clouded with pain.

"Please, dearest, for my sake?"

"It's for your sake I'm going with you."

"They may say something to hurt you," he pleaded.

"I don't think they will," she said as the fire suddenly flashed from her brown eyes.

"But they will, my love, they will. It's hard enough for me. They mustn't hurt you—I can hear them out there now—that black mob—waiting to hoot and yell—please, don't go with me!"

Stella left his cell door, stepped to the window and looked out. Steve Hoyle was passing along the lines of Negroes ranged on either side of the walk, instructing them what to say. He had massed around the door a mob of two hundred to follow his lead the moment John appeared.

"Watch me," he said, "and I'll give you the signal. I want you to let him have it square in the face when I raise my hand. I'll stand on the doorstep. I want a laugh first from five hundred black throats—on old-fashioned nigger laugh, long, deep and loud! It'll be a funny sight, I promise you that."

"We watch ye," answered a big buck Negro with a grin.

Stella heard the click of the lock of John's cell with a start and turned to find the deputy marshal standing with a pair of handcuffs.

"We are ready," he said.

John stepped into the corridor, and extended his hands. The deputy snapped the steel on his wrists, and Stella drew the garlands of flowers from the basket.

"You don't mind the flowers—do you officer? I'm going with you."

"Certainly not, m'am," he replied.

John saw that protest was useless, but he gazed at the garlands with amazement.

"What on earth are you going to do, my dear?"

"Just a little trick of love," was the laughing answer.

She wound the flowers around each handcuff, placed in John's hand the enormous bouquet of roses, and not a trace of steel could be seen.

"You can carry them for me," she said, hurrying on before him.

Stella passed suddenly through the jail door to the little brick landing of the steps on which Steve Hoyle stood to give his signal.

Steve started in surprise at her appearance, stammered and flushed, and a murmur of uncertainty ran through the crowd.

In a moment the traitor had recovered himself,

and glancing at Stella with a sneer of triumph, he shouted to his henchmen:

"Say what you please, boys—don't mind the ladies!"

Stella turned her eyes, gleaming with a deadly purpose, straight on Steve, and a revolver flashed from her hand into his face. He dodged, trembled, and crouched against the wall, while she sternly said:

"Now lift your hand or open your mouth, you contemptible sneak and coward!"

A cry of terror swept the dark crowd, and scores broke and fled.

As John appeared in the doorway, Stella turned to the Negroes and in ringing tones cried:

"I dare one of you black loafers to offer a single insult to the man whose love I hold dearer than my life. I'll kill you as I would a dog."

Revolver in hand, with stern set face and flaming eyes she opened the way through which John Graham passed in silence.

At the station a crowd of friends gathered and cheered his departure.

Old Nicaroshinski slipped a hundred dollars in his hand and whispered in broken voice:

"Don't—don't you vorry, me poy, ve'll puild a monumendt to you in de public squvare yedt!"

Stella was allowed to sit by his side in the car,

and as the train started John looked at her a moment through dimmed eyes, and slowly said:

"The glory of this hour has more than paid for all the pain and all the shame a thousand lives could hold!"

And then in low soft accents broken with sobs she confessed to him the story of her love and at the end with trembling lips asked:

"But you can't hate me for it now, can you, my darling?"

For an answer he bent and tenderly kissed her hand, while she felt rather than heard the low passionate words: "I love you—I love you—I love you!"

CHAPTER X

TIME slowly healed the poisoned wounds left by the fierce struggles of Reconstruction. John Graham's case was never decided by the Supreme Court of the United States. Before the day arrived for the test of its appeal to the great tribunal which is the last bulwark of American liberties, he was hastily pardoned, and every man with him who languished in prison pens for similar political offences. The little politicians who had forced through Congress the venomous Conspiracy Acts in violation of the Constitution of the Republic did not dare to allow the Supreme Court the opportunity to overwhelm them with infamy.

The years have brought magic changes to the people of Independence. The growing city has ploughed a new street through the old Graham house and a dozen beautiful homes stand on the site of its wide lawn.

Poetic justice demanded that Steve Hoyle should pay the penalty of his treachery. But Time plays many a joke on Justice. The Honourable Stephen

Hoyle is now one of our fattest, most solemn and most dignified judges of the Federal Courts.

Ackerman's long talks on imaginary cotton mills had one important result. They planted in John Graham's imagination the seeds of fortune. On his return from prison he quit the practice of law and began the manufacture of cotton goods. To please his wife he bought Inwood, whose wide acres of forest extend to the river. Here the Graham Brothers' mills are located.

The Inwood mansion he restored on its original foundations, rebuilding it of native marble behind the stately old Corinthian pillars around one of which the ivy is yet allowed to hang in graceful festoons.

Ackerman, who is the Superintendent of the mills, lives but a stone's throw from Inwood, and every day Susie's and Stella's children play together on the great lawn that still lies hidden in the heart of the ancient woods.

THE END

Printed in the United States
15561LVS00002B/292